WANDERLUST

SKYE WARREN

WANDERLUST

Can love come from pain?

Evie always dreamed of seeing the world, but her first night at a motel turns into a nightmare. Hunter is a rugged trucker willing to do anything to keep her—including kidnapping. As they cross the country in his rig, Evie plots her escape, but she may find what she's been looking for right beside her.

"Skye Warren will take you into the depths of depravity but bring you home, safe in the end."

—Kitty Thomas, author of Comfort Food

Praise for Wanderlust

"Great edge-of-your-seat writing, touching emotional introspection, and enlightening... even in its darkness."

—Maryse's Book Blog

"It was emotionally harrowing yet had bursts of humour, so extremely dark and disturbing yet sensual."

—TotallyBooked Blog

"I love how Ms. Warren is able to make the angst of these two people so real...downright heartbreaking."

—Salacious Reads

"I fell in love with Hunter, not sure if I was supposed to, but I did."

—Sam, E and R's Awesomeness

"And Hunter – you psychotic, tortured and oh-so complex beast of a man...how I adore you! How I would give anything to hear the rumble of your 18-wheeler behind me and the squeal of your brakes beside me."

—Not Now... Mommy's Reading

"I would say this was dark and disturbing... and it kind of was but for me, when it counts, it's a seriously sweet emotional book."

—Dark Reading Room

CHAPTER ONE

The Niagara Falls were formed by glacier activity 10,000 years ago.

A CLASH OF pots and pans came from downstairs. I winced but remained cross-legged on my bed, staring at the assorted items I'd deemed essential. Some clothes, toiletries.

A map.

There was so much I didn't know, so much I hadn't seen. My absence of knowledge had become an almost tangible thing, filling me up, suffocating me until I needed to kick up to the surface just to breathe.

Ironically, my innocence was my mom's explanation for keeping me home. The world was too scary, and I wouldn't even know how to protect myself. To hear her tell it, the streets were filled with ravening men who would attack me as soon as look at me.

That was the anxiety talking. At least that was what the counselor had said before we'd stopped going.

"Evie!" my mother yelled from the kitchen.

It would be three more times before she elevated to

screams. Four before she threw something. Six before she came up to my room, demanding I make her coffee or whatever else she needed.

I'd grown up fast, fumbling with mac and cheese before I was tall enough to see over the pot, explaining away my excess absences to disinterested teachers. In high school, I'd stayed home and studied to get my GED. Two years of correspondence classes through the community college, and I was desperate for any human contact.

I picked up my book, running my fingers over the cool, glossy surface.

The library was one of the few places approved by my mother. I must have read almost every book in that place, living a thousand lives on paper, traveling around the world in eighty days and through the looking glass. I knew about hope and death, about fear and the dignity required to overcome, but only in theoretical constructs of ink and ground tree pulp. That was my irony: to wax poetic about the meaning of life while being unable to do something as simple as pay rent.

Weary of re-reads, I'd wandered into the nonfiction section. I'd picked this one up on a whim, on a joke almost because the title seemed so silly. *Everything You Wanted to Know About Niagara Falls.* Who wanted to know anything about Niagara Falls?

Then I read it.

I snuck back every day for a week, enamored by the descriptions, in awe of the pictures of water rushing, enchanted by the majesty and magic of this place both faraway and someday attainable. My mother didn't let me get a library card, so I'd stolen the book and kept it ever since.

Now the paper was thin and pliable, well-worn from years of turning the pages. The binding was loose, the stitching visible between the cardboard and glue. By now it was probably held together by the clear tape that held the library tags to the spine.

"Happy birthday," I whispered.

My present to myself: to finally see the place I'd been yearning for. The place I'd dreamed about even before I'd gotten the book, for all twenty years of my life. For room to breathe. For freedom.

Even my camera couldn't sustain me. I flipped through the photographs on the digital screen, every single one taken in the house or the yard. Nowadays mom got antsy when I walked over to the park. There were only so many times I could pretend a new angle of the flower pot was artistic instead of just plain pathetic. I wanted to see new things, new places—new people.

I piled everything into my bag. I was far too old for the purple backpack. But then, my body was too old for me. Somewhere in the past five years, I had blossomed into a woman, with full lips and fuller breasts, with hair in places I was almost afraid to touch, except when I just had to at night in my bed, and I did—oh, I did, and it shamed me. I shamed myself with the wetness and the horrible, rippling pleasure around my fingers.

My twentieth birthday. Neither my mother nor I had acknowledged it at breakfast, as if even the mention of passing time would crack the fragile votive that ensconced us.

And now, I would shatter it.

I wouldn't be going around the world or even outside the state—at least not today. But the fear felt huge inside my stomach. Her anxiety was rubbing off on me. I had to get out of here.

Everything fit neatly into my faded backpack, but then I was well-practiced in packing it after having done so at least a dozen times. Each time had ended in screaming, in tears, and in me back upstairs in my room.

Not this time. If I didn't follow through now, I would be stuck here. I'd live here forever.

I'd die here.

Feeling queasy, I slung the bag over my shoulder and headed down the stairs. My mother sat at the kitchen table, her thin robe loosely tied, eyes glassy from the pills. The medicine was supposed to help her, but she never got better—only worse. More fearful, more controlling.

All those chemicals had taken their toll on her body. She looked so tired. The weary shadows around her eyes and tension lines around her lips always made my gut clench. I should be here to protect her. I just couldn't, I couldn't.

I leaned my backpack against the leg of the table and sat down across from her.

"Mama."

Her eyes came into focus. She sighed. "Not this again, Evie."

I swallowed. "Please, Mama, try to understand. I need to see more of the world than these walls."

"What is there to see? Suffering? People starving? Go look at the TV if you want to see the world so badly. You know I'm right."

We used to watch the news together. Every young girl abducted, every college girl who had her drink drugged was somehow a mark against me.

That could have been you, she would say.

Whereas most families might let the tragedy of strangers pass them by like waves, she would catch them, collect them, marking down their names and ages in her notebooks and checking whether they had been found in six months, a year, five years, until I felt like I was drowning in unseen violence.

"I don't want to watch the news. I want to see things for myself. Ordinary things. I want to *be* ordinary. I want to live."

She scowled. "Don't be dramatic. You're living here.

You're safe."

I firmed. "No, Mama. I know you need to stay inside, but just as much, I need to go out into the world. Experience things for myself. And I'm going to. You can't stop me this time."

Her face seemed to crack. Plump tears slipped down her cheeks. "I don't understand why you're talking this way. What have I ever done but protect you?"

Guilt swelled my chest, but I forced it down. I would be strong.

"I can't stay here. I love you, but I just can't stay."

"Evie, Evie, my baby." She clasped her hands together, begging.

I knelt at her feet, taking her hands in mine. I could feel each bone, each tendon beneath the paper-dry skin.

"Please. Give me your blessing to leave. I'll come back to visit. Maybe even move back to town after a while. I need to see something of the world first."

"How are you going to afford it?"

I'd been lucky enough to get a job doing touchups for a small photography studio up the road when I was sixteen. I could do the work from home, and the paychecks were deposited directly in our account—well, technically my mother's account. I wouldn't take that money even if I could, knowing she didn't have another source of income.

I did get a small weekly allowance, though, and had

saved up a hundred and sixty dollars. Not enough to get me all the way to New York, not with paying for gas, food and motels along the way.

"I talked to someone through the college's job placement system. There's an opening at a photography studio up in Dallas."

I'd work there for a while, saving up money and looking for another stop closer to Niagara Falls. That was the plan anyway.

She sniffed. "If you leave, you won't ever come back."

It was a pronouncement, bitter and unyielding.

"I will, I promise—"

"No." She hardened, her tears drying as quickly as they'd come. "I mean it, Evie. You wouldn't be welcome here anymore. You'd be one of *them*."

The paranoia. I knew it was a sickness, but labeling it didn't help me.

"I'm your daughter. Always."

She shoved back from me. "If that were true, you wouldn't leave me. If you leave, you wouldn't be my daughter anymore."

Her words sank into my stomach like a lead weight. No shock, only resignation. Maybe I had always known it would come to this.

"I love you, Mama," I whispered, and it panged with permanence.

As if finally realizing I was serious, her eyes widened, filling with rage.

"You won't last a second out there. Not one goddamn second, you hear me? You have no idea what kinds of things happen out there—"

"I do, Mama. Because you've told me every day that I can remember. Well, do you think nothing bad ever happens here? That I'm safe just because I'm trapped here? What about Allen?"

Her head jerked back as if I'd slapped her, and in a way, I had. We never talked about that, not even to the counselor.

Mama had dated a few men when I was very young, when she still left the house. The last man she dated was Allen. He had been so very understanding of her desire to spend nights at home instead of going out for dates, even if it meant her young daughter was in the way. My mother would take her pills and go to sleep and he would slip into my room.

One night, she caught him in the act. She'd kicked him out of the house the next day, and that fall, I'd stayed home to be homeschooled instead of going to ninth grade.

She had stopped dating altogether. She stopped going outside too. The world was too scary. Well, I was a little scared too, but I was even more terrified of rotting here. At least her isolation had led to me getting my driver's license and the rust bucket I used to get groceries each week. It was a pumpkin turned into a carriage, ready to take me away from here.

I softened my voice. "I'm not mad at you for what happened. It wasn't your fault."

Her nostrils flared. "You ungrateful bitch. I picked you over him. Is this how you pay me back? By leaving?"

I steeled myself. "I'm going now. I'll call in a few days to let you know I'm settled."

A plate landed at my feet like a Frisbee, clattering harmlessly to the floor, shatter-resistant. I slung my backpack over my shoulder and walked to the door. A bowl of oranges spilled around my ankles. A mug thudded against my leg.

She screamed at me, and I kept walking. I wanted to be smug. I was finally getting what I wanted. I had done it. It was a victory. But I couldn't shake the feeling I had left something important behind.

Not all those who wander are lost. I knew that, I believed it, but just now, with my mother sobbing obscenities while I drove away in my ten-year-old Honda, I felt very alone and a little bit lost.

CHAPTER TWO

*The Niagara Falls mark the border of Ontario, Canada
and New York, USA.*

B Y LATE AFTERNOON, I knew I'd taken a wrong turn.
I'd only driven two hundred miles away from
home. The three-lane highway had narrowed to one lane
on either side, flanked by deep ditches and wide fields.

I'd only run occasional weekly errands in my car, and
now I was driving across Texas—which felt as broad and
wide as the world. The signs changed as soon as I left our
small city. Different colors, different markings than the
maps, and I soon found myself turned around and
twisted.

I considered going back but I'd been driving this way
for two hours. By the time I got back to the main
freeway, it would be dark. I might miss it again and
make everything worse. Besides, I was tired, hungry, and
I really had to use the bathroom.

An exit sign had little pictographs for food, gas, and
lodging. I pulled onto a smaller road, also devoid of cars
or buildings. The pavement was smooth enough. The

little reflective lights in the middle were comforting, like maybe I couldn't be too far from civilization if they'd bothered with safety features.

Eventually I saw a complex up ahead, several buildings clumped together with a row of semi-trucks parked by the gas pumps. It looked like an all-in-one business, with hot food specials listed next to the gas prices and a vacancy sign for rooms to let.

Inside the tiny gas station building, a large balding man sat behind the counter while a tiny fan blew directly at his face. He looked me up and down in a way that made my skin crawl.

"How much?"

"I'm sorry?" I stammered.

Somehow, my mind had made a leap to something inappropriate, as if he were asking how much I would charge to have sex with him.

Crazy thought.

"How much gas?" He nodded toward my car at the pump.

I exhaled, feeling silly. Why had I even thought such a dirty thing? I felt bad for doubting him. That was the anxiety talking, secondhand anxiety leftover from all the lectures my mother had ever given me. Brushing off the embarrassing dust of fear, I paid for my gas and rented a room for the night.

Forty dollars made a sizable dent in my small pocket

of cash, but the musty bed and aging particle board furniture would be more comfortable than the back seat of my car. Even better, the door had a thick, shiny lock that looked like it had been replaced recently, as well as a latch that only opened from the inside. After examining all the entry points, I berated myself for paranoia again.

My stomach growled. The soda I had bought wouldn't tide me over all night. Maybe I'd pick up some chips to go with it. My jeans and a T-shirt seemed stale and a little constricting after the long car ride.

I put on a loose-fitting sundress that fell below my knees. It was white and airy, darkening to baby blue at the hem. I had bought it on impulse from the Walmart about a month ago but never worn it before today. My mother would have said it invited men to sin with me. I thought it was pretty and normal, and hopefully it would help me fake my way to confidence. Slipping twenty bucks into my coin purse along with the room key, I set out.

My car cooled in the night air right outside my door, but there was no point driving such a short distance. The buildings of the gas station, the diner, and the motel rooms were nestled together amid a wide expanse of concrete in an even larger plain of empty farmland. The other motel rooms I passed seemed vacant, their windows dark and parking spaces empty.

I felt tiny out here. Would it always be this way now

that I was free? Our seclusion at home had provided more than security. An inflated sense of pride, diminishing the grand scheme of things to raise our own importance. On this deserted sidewalk in the middle of nowhere, it was clear how very insignificant I was. No one even knew I was here. No one would care.

When I rounded the corner, I saw that the lights in the gas station were off. Frowning, I tried the door, but it was locked. It seemed surreal for a moment, as if maybe it had never been open at all, as if this were all a dream.

Unease trickled through me, but then I turned and caught site of the sunset. It glowed in a symphony of colors, the purples and oranges and blues all blending together in a gorgeous tableau. There was no beauty like this in the small but smoggy city where I had come from, the skyline barely visible from the tree in our backyard. This sky didn't even look real, so vibrant, almost blinding, as if I had lived my whole life in black and white and suddenly found color.

I put my hand to my forehead, just staring in awe.

My God, was this what I'd been missing? What else was out there, unimagined?

I considered going back for my camera but for once I didn't want to capture this on film. Part of my dependence on photography had been because I never knew when I'd get to see something again, didn't know when I'd get to go outside again. I was a miser with each image, carefully secreting them into my digital pockets. But now I had forever in the outside world. I could breathe in the colors, practically smell the vibrancy in the air.

A sort of exuberant laugh escaped me, relief and excitement at once. Feeling joyful, I glanced toward the neat row of semi-trucks to the side. Their engines were silent, the night air still. The only disturbance: a man leaned against the side of one, the wispy white smoke from his cigarette curling upward. His face was shrouded in darkness.

My smile faded. I couldn't see his expression, but some warning bell inside me set off. I sensed his alertness despite the casual stance of his body. His gaze felt hot on my skin. While I'd been watching the sunset, he'd been watching me.

When he suddenly straightened, I tensed. Where a second ago I'd felt free, now my mother's warnings came rushing back, overwhelming me. Would he come for me? Hurt me, attack me? It would only take a few minutes to run back to my room—could I beat him there? But all he did was raise his hand, waving me around the side of the building. I circled hesitantly and found another entrance, this one to a diner.

Hesitantly, I waved my thanks. After a moment, he nodded back.

"Paranoid," I chastised myself.

The diner was wrapped with metal, a retro look that was probably original. Uneven metal shutters shaded the green windows, where an OPEN sign flickered.

Inside, turquoise booths and brown tables lined the walls. A waitress behind the counter looked up from her magazine. Her hair was a dirty blonde, darker than mine, pulled into a knot. A thick layer of caked powder and red lipstick were still in place, but her eyes were bloodshot, tired.

"I heard we got a boarder," she said, nodding to me. "First one of the year."

I blinked. It was a cool April night. If I was the first one of the year, then that was a long time to go without boarders.

"What about all the trucks outside?"

"Oh, they sleep in their cabs. Those fancy new leather seats are probably more comfortable than those old mattresses filled with God-knows-what." She laughed at her own joke, revealing a straight line of grayish teeth.

I managed a brittle smile then ducked into one of the booths.

She sidled over with a notepad and pen.

"We don't usually see girls as pretty as you around here. Especially alone. You don't got nobody to look after you?"

The words were spoken in accusation, turning a compliment into a warning.

"Just passing through," I said.

She snorted. "Aren't we all? Okay, darlin', what'll it be?"

Under her flat gaze, I turned the sticky pages of the menu, ignoring the stale smells that wafted up from it. Somehow the breakfast food seemed safest. I hoped it would be easier to avoid food poisoning with pancakes than a steak.

After the waitress took my order, I waited, tapping my fingers on the vinyl tabletop to an erratic beat. I was a little nervous—jittery, although there was no reason to be. Everyone had been nice. Not exactly welcoming, but then I was a stranger. Had I expected to make friends with the first people I met?

Yes, I admitted to myself, somewhat sheepishly. I had rejected my mother's view that everyone was out to get me, but neither was everyone out to help me. I would do well to retain some of the wariness she'd instilled in me. A remote truck stop wasn't the place to meet people, to make lasting relationships. That would be later, once I had started my job. No, even later than that, when I'd saved up enough to reach Niagara Falls. Then I could relax.

When my food came, I savored the sickly sweet syrup that saturated my pancakes. It would rot my teeth, my mother would have said. Well, she wasn't here. A small rebellion, but satisfying and delicious.

The bell over the door rang, and I glanced up to see a man come in. His tan T-shirt hung loose while jeans hugged his long legs. He was large, strong—and otherwise unremarkable. He might have come from any one of those eighteen-wheelers out there, but somehow I knew he'd been the one watching me.

His face had been in the shadows then, but now I could see he had a square jaw darkened with stubble and lips quirked up at the side. Even those strong features paled against the bright intensity of his eyes, both tragic and terrifying. So brown and deep that I could fall into them. The scary part was the way he stared—insolently. Possessively, as if he had a right to look at me, straight in my eyes and down my neckline to peruse my body.

I suddenly felt uncomfortable in this dress, as if it exposed too much. I wished I hadn't changed clothes. More disturbing, I wished I had listened to my mother. I looked back down at my pancakes, but my stomach felt stretched full, clenched tight around the sticky mass I'd already eaten.

I wanted to get up and leave, but the waitress wasn't here and I had to pay the bill. More than that, it would be silly to run away just because a man looked at me. That was exactly what my mom would do.

Back when we still left the house, someone would just glance at her sideways in the grocery store. Then we'd flee to the car where she'd do breathing exercises before she could drive us home. I was trying to escape that. I *had* escaped that. I wouldn't go back now just because a man with pretty eyes checked me out.

Still, it was unnerving. When I peeked at him from beneath my lashes, I met his steady gaze. He'd seated himself so he had a direct line of vision to me. Shouldn't he be more circumspect? But then, I wouldn't know what was normal. I was clueless when it came to public interaction. So I bowed my head and poked at the soggy pancakes.

Once the waitress gave me the bill, I'd leave. Simple enough. Easy, for someone who wasn't paranoid or crazy. And I wasn't—that was my mother, not me. I could do this.

When the waitress came out, she went straight to his table. I drew little circles in the brown syrup just to keep my eyes off them. I couldn't hear their conversation, but I assumed he was ordering his meal.

Finally, the waitress approached my table, wearing a more reserved expression than she had before. Almost cautious. I didn't fully understand it, but I felt a flutter of nerves in my full stomach.

She paused as if thinking of the right words. Or maybe wishing she didn't have to say them. "The man over there has paid for your meal. He'd like to join you."

I blinked, not really understanding. The gentleness of her voice unnerved me. More than guilt—pity.

"I'm sorry." I fumbled with the words. "I've already eaten. I'm done."

"You have food left on your plate. Doesn't matter how much you want to eat anyway." She paused and then carefully strung each word along the sentence. "He requests the pleasure of your company."

My heart sped up, the first stirrings of fear.

I supposed I should feel flattered, and I did in a way. He was a handsome man, and he'd noticed me. Of course, I was the only woman around besides the waitress, so it wasn't a huge accomplishment. But I wasn't prepared for fielding this kind of request. Was this a common thing, to pay for another woman's meal?

It was a given that I should say no. Whatever he wanted from me, I couldn't give him, so it was only a question of letting him down nicely.

"Please tell him thank you for the offer. I appreciate it, I do. But you see, I really am finished with my meal and pretty tired, so I'm afraid it won't be possible for him to join me. Or to pay for my meal. In fact, I'd like the check, please."

Her lips firmed. Little lines appeared between her brows, and with a sinking feeling I recognized something else: fear.

"Look, I know you aren't from around here, but that there is Hunter Bryant." When I didn't react to the name, her frown deepened. "Here's a little advice from one woman to another. There are some men you just don't say no to. Didn't your mama ever warn you about men like that?"

Anxiety swelled in my chest. My mother *had* warned me, so many times, but I hadn't wanted to believe.

No, I refused to believe.

The world wasn't a scary place where a woman had to be afraid. Instead I embraced my annoyance. This was awkward, and I didn't know how to get out of it without insulting him—or her, for not understanding a basic request or doing her job. She had conveyed the question and been given an answer.

I enunciated each word as if she had a hard time understanding, and for all I knew, maybe she did. She certainly wasn't listening to me. "I'm sorry, but I won't be dining with him. I'm finished. Please give me the check, and I'll pay for my own food."

She frowned. "You're a mouthy little thing."

I scooted back a little. I didn't want to be mouthy. I hadn't really meant to offend. But it seemed inevitable. Each small misstep was a blow to my thin confidence. I'd been prepared for the big problems. Finding housing, dealing with money. Driving across the country. Eventually having a boyfriend and figuring out if I could have sex like a normal woman after what had happened. I hadn't counted on my complete lack of social graces. Like a thousand tiny cuts, they were tearing me apart before I'd even gotten to my destination.

"I'm really sorry," I said, and I meant it. Whatever was the right thing to do or say in this moment, I didn't know it.

But I couldn't agree to eating dinner with him, to letting him pay for my meal, and then owing him…what? What was the proper etiquette when a man bought dinner? A goodnight kiss, more? I didn't know that either. But I did know he made me uncomfortable. If I could put my foot in my mouth around this waitress, it would be so much worse around him. Even several booths over, his dark gaze tied my tongue in knots.

"I can't," I whispered, trying to convey to her the urgency of my situation. The impossibility of it.

"Have it your way." A strange light entered her eyes, like one of remembrance. "Maybe you have the right idea anyway. It always ends the same way. Might as well hold onto control as long as you can."

Her words sent a chill down my spine.

I fumbled with my coin purse. "I don't need the bill. Here, this should cover it."

The twenty dollar bill I left was more than the total should have been, even with a tip, and I couldn't really spare any money but neither could I stay there another minute, pinned by his gaze and terrified by the ancient pain in hers.

Pointedly avoiding looking at him, I slipped out the

door and scurried along the broken concrete until I reached my room. I shut the door, twisting the heavy deadbolt to lock it.

CHAPTER THREE

*The first person to see and describe Niagara Falls in depth
was a French priest who accompanied an expedition
in 1678.*

M Y SKIN STILL prickled as I huddled in my motel
room—something about him had been off. The
way the man had looked at me, unflinching, unnerving,
had tripped off all sorts of animal instincts inside me that
I couldn't precisely interpret except to know to avoid
him.

I latched the little hook on the door for good meas-
ure. Glancing sideways at the heavy drapes, I sent silent
thanks for the metal burglar bars on the window.

In the diner, where even the waitress had seemed
intimidated, I'd felt vulnerable. But now I was well and
truly encased in the motel room, where I would stay
until morning. It felt a little like failure, falling back on
my old ways, but I considered it only a temporary
retreat. Things would be different in Little Rock and
even that was only until I'd saved enough money to
continue north.

A shower was the next order of business, so I headed across the shadowed room and bumped directly into the round dinette table.

"Ouch," I muttered.

Had that been directly aligned with the door before? I wasn't even sure where the light switches were. It had been daylight when I'd first been in the room, with the sunlight streaming through the window…through the open drapes. Now they were closed. I had seen that clear enough even in the darkness, the vertical lines where the barred window had once been visible.

A shiver ran through me. Who had closed the curtains? Had someone been in my room while I'd eaten?

Housekeeping. It must have been the maid service. Please, God, let it have been them.

I stood frozen in fear and indecision for a moment before forcing myself forward. The cool vinyl wall met my outstretched palms, and I fumbled until I found the switch. It flicked up with a click, flooding the bathroom with a blinding yellow light.

My heart thumped wildly for one moment as all the things my terrified imagination had conjured didn't happen. Nothing but an empty, dingy, slightly dirty motel bathroom. A shower with a questionably yellowed shower curtain, a sink, a toilet. No beasts or monsters in sight. No scary men with ill intent.

I spared a glance for the room, now lit faintly by the

spill of light from the bathroom. The bed was made, my bag still sitting on top, gaping open from where I had pulled the dress out earlier. The table and chair sat in the empty space between the bed and the wall, obtrusive for the blind and clumsy like me.

I was freaking myself out with this. No, he had done that. The man at the diner with his too-knowing gaze. Well, he was pushy and inappropriate, and I was done being scared of strangers.

The tile was cool against my bare feet. I undressed quickly, finding relief in the warm water that rained on my skin. I even used the bitter-smelling soap wrapped up in paper, comforted by the intensity, feeling cleansed of the man's presence and safe again. More importantly, I was free. Independent. Exactly what I had always longed to be—though I had little experience with it. Maybe that was what made me so jumpy. Maybe he was a normal man, a nice one, and I had jumped to conclusions.

I had always considered myself self-reliant. I'd had to be with my mother. I cooked for myself when my mom was on a binge. I got dressed for school and took the bus, otherwise a child-protective-services woman would come around and we'd all get in trouble. As soon as I was able, I took the part-time job at the photography studio.

All that self-sufficiency, but it wasn't the same as being truly alone. My mom had always been around the house. Even when I'd desperately wished for privacy, for a brief respite from her clinging, cloying fear, I'd never gotten it. Now I was on my own and I'd have to get used to that, somehow. That was what I wanted...wasn't it?

The thin motel towel turned soggy after a couple swipes at my skin. I examined myself in the mirror. Pale blonde hair that looked golden when wet. Light brown eyes that looked hazel in a certain light. I thought those were my best feature but my one boyfriend from high school had thought it was my lips. Kissable, he'd said.

Then the other man, later, had been less diplomatic, more succinct. Fuckable. I had flinched, instinctively knowing what he meant even though I shouldn't have. My mother's lists of abducted girls had never been specific about what had happened to them. Sex was a vague concept for someone who had only ever been kissed after homeroom. But then she had dated Allen, and he had said my lips were made for kissing a place other than his lips, lower down, and he'd taught me how to do it, again and again.

At first I had gone along with it, too afraid of setting my mother off with a confession. But then he'd gotten rougher, more forceful and scary and also tingly hot in ways I didn't fully understand. One evening when he wasn't there, I had tried to tell my mother what was happening.

I'd expected her to help me. After all, she'd always told me something like that could happen at any time.

But she hadn't believed me. She'd said I was making up stories, that I wanted the attention those girls on the news had gotten. That I was jealous of the time she spent with Allen and that must be why I had made up such lies.

I cried into my pillow and let Allen do his business that night. But the light had turned on, a flood of painful light, and my mother had seen. After that, she'd apologized for not believing me.

She'd been kind, understanding. Too understanding, and that had been the final straw. She'd quit her job, claiming she needed to stay home and watch me, that the world was too dangerous for either of us. Especially me.

She said I attracted them, the very worst kind of men. And maybe she was right to a point. There was something there, something large and scary lurking under the water. Every once in a while it would surface with a flip of my stomach, like when a man would speak to me with a certain authority, give me an order—or a certain look, like the one in the diner.

I didn't like it, or maybe I liked it too much, but I couldn't stand being like my mother. I wouldn't end up like her, broken and lonely and so desperate for any man that I'd put up with someone like Allen. That was why I'd had to leave home, why I insisted on getting a college education. This was my ticket away from a life of subservience and fear.

Well then, why did I feel so afraid? But the wide-eyed girl in the mirror didn't have an answer.

With the towel still wrapped around my body, I stepped out of the bathroom onto the coarse carpet of the motel room. Immediately I knew something was horribly wrong. The air felt... shared.

"Nice to meet you, Evie," said a deep voice.

My whole body strung up tight. He was sitting in the chair, the one that had been empty when I'd gone into the bathroom. It was him, the man from the diner. Though I hadn't heard his voice before and I couldn't quite make out his features now, I was sure of it. He had the same blithe arrogance, the same element of command—sure his word would be followed. Besides, how many psycho assholes could there be in a remote truck stop?

His silhouette was long and reclined, as if he were having a relaxing chat instead of breaking and entering. My gaze flicked to the door, but the deadbolt was sideways, unlocked, when I was sure I'd locked it.

Always lock the door, my mother said. I had scoffed. Who would come in?

Here was my answer.

Nausea roiled through me. "How did you get inside?"

It wasn't the most important question, and we both knew it. What was he going to do to me? That was the bottom line, but I couldn't let my mind go there just yet.

His broad shoulders shrugged. "I've been coming around here for years. The owner is a personal friend. I explained I had some unfinished business in this room, and he gave me a key."

So easy, that was all I could think. My safety, my life had been compromised with a shrug.

How could I get out of this? I couldn't. I knew that with the same certainty that I knew my mother would die in that house. But I had to try. I knew what he meant by unfinished business. He was offended by my refusal earlier. It wouldn't help to pretend I didn't know.

"I'm sorry I didn't accept your offer," I said, hating the note of pleading in my voice, the tremble that betrayed me. "I should have. It was rude of me."

"Very pretty," he said. "And you got there so quickly. I'm impressed."

I tried to pretend that was promising. "Please. I wouldn't... I won't do it again. Maybe tomorrow we could try again. We could go on a date, you and I."

"Tomorrow you'll be gone from here and so will I. But you can stop talking about the bill. I would be in this room either way. I knew it as soon as I saw you there."

Any hope of talking my way out of this deflated. He was sitting between me and the door, but even if I got past him, it would take several precious seconds to open the door. Then outside, there was no one around. My room was in the back. All the windows around me had been dark. My car sat alone in the lot.

No one would see me run. No one would hear me scream.

He waited with a smug patience, as if he waited for me to catch up to the forgone conclusion.

"Are you ready to cooperate?" he asked.

Hell no. My lips firmed.

He smiled, white teeth glistening from the shadows. He looked the Cheshire cat, that incorporeal grin, the unapologetic wickedness.

Except he hadn't done anything to me.

So far he'd just sat in my room. Disturbing but not harmful. He'd done nothing illegal, if I didn't count trespassing. All I had to do was walk out the door and leave. March straight to the office and demand a refund. A laugh wanted to bubble out of me, but I forced it down, knowing it would border on hysterical. This was only the rambling of a terrified mind trying to make sense of things that didn't make sense, desperate to feel safe while so obviously in abject danger.

He hadn't threatened me explicitly, but it was there. In his presence, in his casually arrogant words. If I tried to leave, he would restrain me. He would hurt me tonight, violate me tonight, the only question left up to me was how much. If I cooperated, would he be gentle with me? But it was too soon. I couldn't bring myself to submit to this yet even if it might make my life easier.

I edged toward the phone on the nightstand.

He leaned forward. "What are you doing?"

"Just…just calling the front desk." I forced a challenge in my voice. "If he gave you the key, then it shouldn't be a surprise to him."

It was a long shot, of course. If the manager had given him the key, he was an accomplice to whatever this was. But maybe if he heard my voice…if I seemed more human reaching out over the phone line, more scared, he might do something to help me.

I gingerly lifted the bulky plastic receiver as if it might bite. As if he might spring into action, finally revealing the violence that must be his intent. Instead he watched, eyes glittering while I listened to dead air. The line had been cut. Or maybe it had never worked. He seemed to expect that.

My hand trembled so hard that the phone clattered on the cradle before sliding to the side, useless, broken.

My voice cracked. "Please. I don't know what you want from me."

"Don't you?"

I drew myself up. "You need to leave. I'm not going to…have sex with you."

My words hung in the air, somehow worse now that I'd voiced them, as if I were the one suggesting it instead of him. He was as still as a deep pool, a limitless source of patience, allowing me to work myself up into panic while he watched in amusement.

"Enough," I said, more firmly. "You want to sit there? Fine. I'm leaving."

Clutching the towel to me, I strode to the door. I flipped the lock but before I reached the latch, his heavy palm came up against the door. He didn't block the latch or the knob. He simply leaned his weight, his thickly muscled bulk against the door and waited. This close, I could smell the faint scent of aftershave, of musk at the end of the day. His heat seeped into my back, electrifying and strangely comforting after the cold chills of fear.

"Let me go." The command came out soft, a plea.

"I'm not doing anything to you," he said. "Yet."

I was confined by the unopenable door to my front, penned in by his broad body from behind. Well and truly trapped, and he hadn't even touched me yet. I wondered if that was the game. Maybe he was waiting for me to push him, to strike him. Then he could say his actions were self-defense, in whatever twisted mental world he lived in.

My throat felt tight. "I don't want to fight you."

"Then don't. I think you know what I want. Do I need to spell it out for you? Ask me to."

I swallowed. "What do I have to do for you to leave?"

"I'm going to spend the night here and we're both going to have a good time. In the morning, I'm leaving."

He spoke with authority, but there was a question

inherent. Only one unknown. This was happening, but would I fight him?

God, I didn't know.

I didn't know if I could let this happen without a fight. I didn't know if I could fight him, knowing I would lose, that I would only end up hurt. I saw my mother's face, drawn and worried and accusing. Had this been her choice to make too?

Maybe he knew I was close because he continued, the low timbre of his voice rough and thick.

"I don't get off on hurting women. Not too bad anyway. If you have any bruises they'll be small and covered up by your clothes. No one needs to know what happened here. It's nobody's business but ours."

He made it sound consensual. But that was what he was describing, wasn't it? That I go along with this, that I would consent.

Or else.

And I was too scared to ask about what "or else" would mean.

"Oh God," I sobbed against the peeling paint of the door. "I didn't bother you. You're a good-looking guy. You could get a regular date. Why are you doing this?"

"Thank you for the compliment. You're a pretty girl too. We'll be good together. This is a date, you and I. You wanted to skip the dinner part, and I allowed it. I'm not going to miss dessert."

CHAPTER FOUR

The three waterfalls combine to produce the highest flow rate of any waterfall on earth.

A SICK SENSE of inevitability slid down my throat. Maybe this was a regular date—what did I really know of courtship? He seemed very certain. And maybe it was a self-fulfilling prophecy. If I agreed to this crazy proposition, if I didn't fight him, it would be just a man and a woman having sex. Wouldn't that be better than the alternative? Even without an explicit threat, plain old mildly-bruising sex had to be better than what he might do in anger.

Unable to submit, I searched desperately, trying to think of something that could help. But I was in the far corner of a deserted motel in a truck stop well off the highway. I had no practical experience to guide me, only empty words on musty pages. Like Alice, I had stepped through the looking glass into a whole new world, foreign and sinister.

The old rules didn't apply to this musky hotel room. There was only this man, strong and confident. There was only his mercy, to be gained through pleasing him, not angering him.

"You're thinking too much," he said, and I heard the first rise of frustration in his voice. His patience had a limit after all, and it was approaching on the horizon.

"Please, please," I whispered. "Is there something else I could...anything else...?"

He scoffed. "What else could I want from you?"

Nothing. There was nothing at all, no pride, no hope.

"There now." His voice softened. Something stirred my hair. His hand stroked down, then toyed with a damp lock. "You're making this a bigger deal than it needs to be. It doesn't mean anything, you and I. Just casual sex. Have you had casual sex before?"

No, never. I shook my head.

He seemed amused, a little pleased. "So this will be your first time, in a way. I like that. It's a turn-on."

His fingertips drifted over my bare shoulders, leaving a trail of goose bumps in languid circles. I hugged the door, suddenly wishing that I were the kind of woman who had casual sex. That I could turn around and let the towel drop and pretend I wanted this too. It would make this easier. Instead I could only shiver against the door, shudder under his touch.

"Lock the door," he murmured against my ear. "I don't want to be interrupted."

I took a deep breath and tried to calm myself.

There are some men you just don't say no to. That was what the waitress had said to me, and I understood it now. I wouldn't say no, and he wouldn't force me. I would go along with it, and everything would be consensual.

Just like a date. Casual sex.

My hand shook violently as I reached up and turned the lock sideways. It didn't change our situation at all. I couldn't leave before it was locked, and I still couldn't. But it felt different, as if I had exercised my choice. As if I'd consented, and I had. He had my permission, even though he'd proven he didn't need it.

He trailed his hand down my arm, wrapping his fingers around my wrist. Even though he only touched me in one place, it felt intimate. Though he didn't squeeze, I felt fragile. Breakable.

Leading me to the bed, he pushed me gently to sit. I tightened the towel around myself, and he let me. I'd expected him to push me down, to tear the towel off and have sex with me. But I always seemed to overestimate his penchant for force. It was something about his presence, brute strength combined with the cunning to use it well. He wasn't afraid of violence but neither was he overly fond of it. Or maybe that was just wishful thinking.

He sat down beside me, his light caresses still restricted to my arms, my shoulders. Safe places, as if we were still getting acquainted. As if my comfort mattered at all.

"Tell me about your boyfriends," he said.

"What d-d-do you want to know?"

Oh no. I hadn't stuttered since I was a kid. My mother had tried to frighten it out of me, but that only made it worse. Eventually I'd grown out of it...right around the time I'd gotten my book on Niagara Falls. Now my dreams deserted me along with my composure.

He raised his eyebrow, a sign he had heard my stutter, but he made no comment on it. Instead he asked, "How many have you had? How far did you let them go with you?"

I thought the phrasing was odd, even if it was technically accurate. How far I let them go, like he recognized my dominion over my body. Maybe he considered this the same thing; maybe it was. I was letting him do it to me. I was letting this happen.

Swallowing, I said, "My first boyfriend was in eighth grade. We only dated for a few months and never really saw each other outside school."

"Did you fuck him?"

The question was blunt, and I flinched. "No. We d-didn't do that. We would meet sometimes, outside the school during gym class."

"You made out." He smirked.

The arrogant action didn't subtract from his attractiveness; it enhanced it. Up close, I realized he was one of the most handsome men I'd ever met. I never would have looked at him twice, mostly because of his age. He looked about ten years older than me. I never would have expected him to look twice at me either, but then I had always worn baggy clothes and hung at the edges of a crowd with my mother before we made a quick exit.

"Did you let him touch your tits?

"Yes."

"Under your shirt or just over?"

"Over at f-first. And then he started—" I broke off as he touched my breasts through the towel, just two fingers on the top slope, then around the underside.

"He started what?" he prompted, still stroking, soft caresses on the rough fabric.

I swallowed, willing myself not to tremble. "Then he started reaching under my clothes."

He tugged the towel down. I loosened my hold, letting the cloth slide down my breasts. The hem of the towel caught on my nipples, baring the slope of my breasts but no more. It was almost more obscene this way than if I'd been naked, but I couldn't bring myself to pull the towel down.

Instead I stared into the darkness at the shadowy curtains that I hadn't drawn closed while the weight of the wet towel tugged at the tender skin of my nipples. He drew his finger over the tops of my breasts.

I sucked in deep breaths, more panicked now, everything more sensitive, so acute—like pain. He touched me so lightly, and it hurt. How would it feel when he was rough? Because surely he would be. There was only one reason I could think of why a man who looked as good as he did would force a woman—because he preferred it that way.

"Why did you let him, your boyfriend? Surely you worried about being caught? I bet he didn't even give you an orgasm out back behind the school. Were you that desperate for a skinny eighth-grader?"

His words knocked the breath from me. "No, I just... He wanted to, that's all. I figured it didn't hurt anything just to let him."

"That's right," he said approvingly, soothingly. "It doesn't hurt anything to just let him."

With a flick of his fingers, the towel slipped off my nipples, gaping open around my waist. I sucked in a breath and shut my eyes.

"Just let it happen," he murmured. "I want to do this. You let that little kid paw at you, so why not me?"

His warm hand closed around one breast. It was lifted, hefted into his palm before he rolled the nipple between callused fingers. It didn't hurt anymore. He was right about that. It felt good, the slight abrasiveness, the pressure.

Sparks set off low in my belly. He played with my

breasts with a proficiency that made my breath catch. Clearly he was experienced. He knew just where to touch me and how to do it. But he seemed to be learning me as well, exploring every dip, every milky expanse of skin and the pink tips that pebbled under his manipulation. My hands were tense by my sides, my eyes shut tightly until he pinched my nipple. I gasped.

"Did he do that?"

"No, I—"

"What else did you let him do? Where else did you let him put his skinny little fingers?"

He made it sound so dirty, when it had just been innocent exploration between two teenage kids, hadn't it? That was normal. *This* was the fucked-up thing.

He twisted my nipple when I didn't answer.

I sucked in a breath at the pain. "I don't know—*oh God.*"

"Your cunt? Did he touch you there?"

His coarse words made my face heat. I couldn't remember ever hearing that word aloud but I knew what it meant. Maybe it was just a universal sound or the tone he used, derisive and eager in one note.

"No," I said. "Sometimes his hands would slip under my jeans, but only in the back."

"He touched your ass. That's it? That's all he got to do to you?"

Cheeks burning, I nodded.

"No wonder that didn't last. What about the next boyfriend? Did you put out for him?"

My voice fell to a whisper. "There wasn't...He wasn't..."

"Tell me about the big day. Were there rose petals and candles?"

The pain washed over me afresh. Romance? Not likely. I cursed my mother all over again for not seeing through him, for not seeing how much I was hurting in those weeks before she discovered us.

"He wasn't my boyfriend."

"Ah, now that is interesting. Where were you the first time, in his car?"

"In my room."

"What did he have you do?"

"He said to... I was on my hands and knees."

He whistled. "He came at you from behind for your first time. That's harsh. I don't think I would've even done it that way. Did you come like that, with your face hugging the sheets?"

I shook my head quickly.

It had hurt so bad. He'd stabbed deep inside, and I hadn't known how to control the depth at all, had been too afraid and cowed to fight back. I hadn't been able to, with his hands on my hips, holding me steady for his thrusts. The floral fabric of the comforter turned damp beneath my cheeks as I cried in pain, but he told me to quiet down.

The first always hurts, he'd whispered.

That was in the past. The horrible memory wasn't relevant to me anymore. Except this man pulled me down to the fraying floral bedspread. The towel remained in a limp heap where I had sat, leaving my body completely exposed. I shut my eyes tightly, but I could see the scene as clearly as if we were in broad daylight. My body awkwardly splayed across the bed, tense and vulnerable. He still fully clothed, wearing jeans and a blue button-down.

I felt my hands pulled above my head.

"I wouldn't treat you that way," he said. "The first time is something special."

The sleek sound of leather whipped through the air. I cringed, anticipating the blow.

He soothed me with a stroke of my thigh, as if I were an animal. Gentle hands wrapped the smooth leather around my wrists and secured them to the headboard with an ease that scared me.

"You can get out of that," he said, nodding toward my tethered hands. "If something were to happen, you could wriggle and yank them out. It's safe."

Safe? Was that really a consideration here? This whole thing was unsafe. That was too mild a word. It was devastating.

A tear slipped down my cheek. "Why?"

His face darkened. "We aren't back to that again, are we?"

"Please," I babbled. "I won't tell anyone. Just don't hurt me, please."

He pulled a knife from his pocket. My eyes widened and I squirmed. Instead of using it on me, he cut a strip of the damp towel and slanted it over my mouth, tying it behind my head.

At my pleading look, he shook his head sadly. "We had an agreement. You can't just change your mind. There's a word for girls who do that."

A low, mournful sound left my throat.

"Is that really what you want, girl? To make me angry? To leave me with this?" He gestured jerkily to his crotch, at the bulge in the denim.

I shook my head—no, no. I didn't want him to be angry.

"That's right. It will be okay. You let boyfriend number one touch your tits. You let non-boyfriend number two fuck your cunt. Now you're going to let the dangerous stranger you met on a road trip tie you up and fuck you. It's a fantasy, sunshine. Just a dream."

Though it seemed very real when he stood and took off his clothes. I couldn't see very clearly in the dark, just angled shadows and sleek lines. A light dusting of hair on dusky skin. My vision was blurry, but I felt his presence, touched by the hawk-like gaze on my body and battered by his arousal pulsing in the air.

I couldn't move my hands. I couldn't talk. So I tried not to think either. I wanted to become a purely physical being, one who could feel and be felt but didn't have to analyze any of it. Why had I ever agreed to this? How much of this was my fault and how much his? But if I were just a body, then it didn't matter. If I were just a warm tumble of limbs and curves tacked against the bed, an unholy amenity in this godforsaken motel, then it couldn't be my fault. I could just let it happen.

He touched his palm to the inside of my thigh, and I let it fall open. The idea of refusal was ludicrous now, with all of my power taken from me, all willingly forfeited in a game I'd been destined to lose. But he didn't enter me with that dark, thick erection that jutted from between his legs. He leaned down and breathed in deep. A soft tingle ran up my core. He lapped at me with a tenderness that hurt worse than violence. The first time a man had ever done this to me, and it was against my will. But how could this be against my will, when I wanted it so very badly? It felt so good, so right, like huddling up to a campfire on a winter's night.

I panted into the towel cutting across my mouth. My breasts heaved obscenely, the small twin mounds obscuring the sight of him below, leaving only a half-circle of dark hair between my thighs. He pushed a finger inside me, the intrusion so stark that I grunted.

"Ah fuck," he said. "I meant to make you come this way, but you're so tight. I need to be inside you."

He reached for his pants and grabbed a small packet—a condom, something I felt thankful for at least. I was aroused from the illicitness of the situation and from his tongue on my cunt, but not so far gone that I lost my sense of self. I wanted to get out of this safely. That had to be my goal.

When he leaned back over me, his cock sheathed and breathing labored, I cringed back.

"No, pretty girl." He rained kisses over my forehead, on my nose. "You want this, don't you? You want this cock inside you. You're all the same."

I bit down on the towel, unable to answer. I was almost thankful for the gag in that moment, because what could I say? I may have gone along with this, but I hadn't really wanted it. This wasn't something I had chosen.

"Please," he said.

It was a role reversal, him begging instead of me. He wanted me to do more than allow his use of me, he wanted me to want this too. I couldn't though, and it wouldn't matter anyway. If I said no, what then? He was unpredictable even when I cooperated. I didn't want to make him angry.

I nodded quickly.

Unappeased, he pulled the towel down from my

mouth. "Say it."

"I want your cock inside me," I said in a deadened voice. It didn't even sound like me. I had gotten my wish. I was purely physical—a machine with no emotions. Skin with no heart.

His face twisted into a sneer. "I don't believe you."

"Please put your cock inside me. I want you to fuck me."

He sat back on his heels, his cock rising between us. "Fuck. You're not even a good liar."

Letting my eyes fall shut, I finally spoke the truth. "Make me come. Please. Show me what it could be like if a man could make me come."

The bed rocked gently as he leaned back over me, though I couldn't look at him. I couldn't see the smugness again, the triumph. A blunt head fitted to my opening. I gasped and writhed on the bed. It felt too large. It had been so long.

In a sudden stroke, he entered me, stretching my walls wide and far. I cried out, helpless to quiet the pain that wrenched me in half. He didn't give me time to adjust, just pulled out and slammed back in. Tears ran in rivulets down my face. Stunned, I realized it wasn't the pain that made me cry, or the violation, but the betrayal. He'd said he wouldn't be like before, but this was the same. It was hard and painful and fast.

"So fucking tight," he said, panting. "You're going to

come for me."

I shook my head. Just another betrayal, that empty promise. I would spread my legs for him, but I wouldn't fake it.

He wouldn't even notice if I did. Despite his words, he was far away, his gaze focused on the horizon of his own pleasure. The look on his face was pure ecstasy, his movement jerky and desperate. It stirred me, his need, enough that I felt myself twinge around his cock.

At the contraction, his breath caught. There was a pause, a heartbeat of tortured stillness. Like a dammed force unleashed, he sped up, thrusting wildly. A long, pained sound escaped him, punctuated by his grunts as he forced himself deeper and faster.

His mouth sought out my skin as if it were sustenance, as if it were air. He drew open-mouthed kisses along my collarbone, my neck, breathing me in. I could feel the secret muscles tightening and convulsing. In a sort of feedback loop, his harsh plunder forced them to quiver. The vibrations sent him even higher, spurred him ever faster. It turned the tables too. I was bound and spread open but he was helpless to the squeeze of my sex, to the lure of my skin.

He rammed into me, pulling me down onto his body as if I were a toy, a tool, something to be used well and then put away.

His eyes glazed over. "Oh God."

He reared up over me, so that all I saw was a blur of hard-packed shoulders. His whole body was racked by the force of each entry, as if he were a ship battered up against rocks. I feared for him then, maybe more than myself. It was almost inhuman, the rage with which he fucked me, the tempest of his lust, and yet wholly vulnerable. Fierce and thick and uncontrollable—neither of us were master now.

My pain became his, twisting his face into a mask of helpless agony. Every jolt of my inner muscles, every slap of flesh against flesh was reflected in his eyes. He stared at me, some of the intensity slipping, reflecting back fear. What was he afraid of?

Tears streamed down my face. Didn't he like it? Wasn't this what he wanted?

"It's okay," I whispered.

He spoke with grunts. "Shut up."

"Let it happen." The words were a mockery, but they were the truth.

He barely paused in his wild thrusts, as he reached up to slap my face. I blinked against the sting. My head jerked against the pillow, and he held it there, stretching away from my body as if he could separate it, as if he could split my mind from my body, and God, if he could have, it would have been a mercy. I didn't want to think or feel—but I did. It was inevitable, and I knew what he needed with the bone-deep certainty. There were so few things we knew for sure, and mercy was one of them.

Shutting my eyes against the dark, I whispered, "I forgive you."

His body stuttered, halted suddenly in a harsh and rigid climax. He jerked my head back and mashed his lips against mine, sucking and biting at me with a violence that triggered my own orgasm. I came with long inner pulls of his twitching cock and a quiet cry that tumbled onto his tongue.

As our bodies softened and cooled in the aftermath, he stared at me, almost bewildered.

A slow blink brought awareness and a glimmer of wonder. His mouth curved in a sleek, satisfied smile.

He bent his head and licked my bottom lip. "I liked that very much."

For reasons I couldn't analyze, his words made my sex clench around his softened cock.

He chuckled and rolled to the side.

With leisurely movements, he untied me. I rubbed my wrists for a moment, unsure about what to do. I could make a run for it. There would never be a better chance than right now. But it felt overly dramatic. I had my things on the bathroom counter and a fifty dollar deposit at the front desk. It hadn't hurt. It was only casual sex. In fact, it was the best sex I'd ever had. The only consensual sex, if I could call it that.

Leaning over, I pulled the condom off, using my

hand to keep it from spilling. He jerked in my hand then grunted.

"What are you doing?" he muttered.

I cocked my head. "Cleaning you. Isn't that...? I thought..."

He sent me a lazy grin. "Let me guess. Boyfriend number two."

"He wasn't my boyfriend."

"Well he sounds like one hell of a bastard, but it seems I owe him one." He gestured to himself. "Get to it then."

I turned back to my task, licking up the salty juices from his softening cock, his balls, working my tongue down into the taint as I had been taught to. It had tasted copper with my blood then. It was the way between a man and a woman, he'd said, and I had never questioned the practice until now. Still, it seemed to satisfy this man too. He let out a small sigh as I ran my tongue from the tip of his cock to the base.

When I had cleaned him, he pushed my head gently down against his stomach. His abs were hard and lightly-furred—an unconventional pillow. Exhausted from the fear and the struggle, sated from climax, I slipped into a dark sleep.

I dreamed of my mother. Her face was distorted and twisted.

She sneered at me. "Not so proud now, are you?"

"I didn't want to do it," I sobbed. "He made me."

"You left just so you could fuck guys like him."

"No, no." I pleaded for her to understand, for her to absolve me. "I didn't know."

"With that face and that body?" she scoffed. "You knew what would happen, and you wanted it."

"Why didn't you stop me?"

"I did, girl. I told you not to go…not to go…"

I woke up with a cock in my mouth. I gasped, struggling to breathe. It took me a few minutes and several thrusts to get oriented. My hands were tied behind my back, arching my body up as I lay on top of them. He straddled my neck, thrusting mercilessly into my mouth. He didn't seem to notice that I was awake now, or care that I had been asleep before. He simply used me, and something subversive sent warmth to…to my cunt. That was what he called it. But there was nothing but cool air between my legs as he sawed his cock against my tongue.

I tried to use my tongue, to find the rhythm, but it was erratic, only in his head. I could do nothing but open to him, to take him repeatedly until he grunted and filled my mouth with foamy cum. A drop spilled out of the corner of my mouth and trailed down my skin. There were no tears left, only this.

He sighed as he slipped out. Sleepily, almost as if he were still sleeping, he scooted down my body until his head rested on the cushion of my breasts. They were soft and plump, but they couldn't have made a comfortable pillow. Still, he fell asleep almost instantly, his breathing evening out into a peace I could only envy.

Blinking up at the water-stained ceiling, I wondered if I could pretend this night had never happened.

I must have drifted off to sleep, because when I woke, my arms were in agony. He used me many times that night. He dragged me onto his cock, forcing me to ride him while my arms were still bound behind me. He controlled the speed of my thrusts with twists and slaps to my breasts. The next time he licked at my cunt, sucked and bit until I came with a screaming abandon I'd never felt or even imagined.

The next time he dragged me by my hair to the bathroom where the bright light stung my sleep-dimmed eyes. He scrubbed my body with the harsh soap, as if to remove every trace of him. Then he took me back to the bed, spread me open, and sprayed ropes of cum across my breasts, ruining all his work.

There was an inconsistency there, as if he were fighting himself just to fuck me. I started to fear that he would kill me after all. Maybe it would get to be too much. Maybe we were stuck in an infinite loop of lust and hatred, and the only way to end it would be to kill me. Which would I prefer—to spend an eternity in purgatory or take a gamble with hell? But these were only the meandering thoughts of an exhausted mind, because this would end soon. Already morning light whispered through the curtains. Our sex had turned sluggish and sloppy, though he seemed reluctant to end it.

I knelt, my face and shoulders pressed into the coverlet as he pushed into me from behind. When he came, his groan sounded like an animal in agony, a cry for help. He jerked back his cock, and I knew it was as sensitive and raw as my own tender flesh. It didn't make sense why he pushed himself to the pain, but we weren't operating on the laws of logic here, not inside the looking glass. There was only our primal senses, a sort of ironic inevitability, like an animal who fights to the death just to prove that he's dominant.

I dozed on the bed, too broken to move, as I heard him get up and rummage around the room. The sink in the bathroom went on briefly. There was the sound of water nearby, and then he was raising my head, tilting it up. The curve of a cup touched my lips. Cool water slid down my parched throat, following by a bitter aftertaste and powder residue.

I made a face and tried to pull away.

"Shh," he said, nudging the cup against my lips. "Drink up."

My limbs were too heavy to push him and already the liquid ran down my neck. I opened my mouth and drank. Relief filled me.

"That's a good girl." He leaned down, whispering

into my ear. "I'm sorry about this. I really am. You're too good."

He'd really done it, I realized as my consciousness faded. He'd killed me, and now we could both be free.

CHAPTER FIVE

The Niagara Falls State Park is the oldest state park in the United States.

I WOKE UP in a rumbling, rattling darkness. My body was jolted around. I heard the hollow bang of metal, but some sort of thin padding protected me from the worst of the blows. Every time I tried to move, pain seared through my brain. As blood returned to my fingers and toes, agony followed. So I focused on staying as still as possible, eyes shut tightly against the possibility that was becoming more and more certain.

The back of a truck. I was in *his* truck.

He hadn't killed me. He'd been apologizing for kidnapping me. It wasn't hard to figure out what I would be used for. This was a nightmare, exactly the kind of thing my mother warned me about. I would take all of the precautions she wanted while secretly rolling my eyes because that kind of thing only happened to girls on TV. Not to me. Oh God, not to me.

Whether from remnants of the drug or just fear, I felt exhausted, and I allowed the steady motion of the truck to lull me into a thoughtless place. Nothing so comforting as sleep, but free of the nightmares my mind drew for me. Last night had only been the beginning. There was more.

Slowly, almost reluctantly, I took inventory of my body. My hands were tied behind my back, cuffed at the wrists by something soft but intractable. My feet were similarly bound, though I couldn't see them at all. I was lying on something mildly soft, maybe a padding or a thick blanket.

And I was naked. Of course I was naked and damp and aching down there where he had entered me. I didn't even know what to call that place. My vagina. That seemed wrong, too clinical. A gasping, desperate laugh escaped me. I could barely put a name to it, but he'd been inside there. Inside my cunt.

My innocence suddenly seemed sinister, as if it were the true cause of my predicament. Maybe if I'd had more experience with men, I would have anticipated this. If I'd had regular sex, I would be able to handle this.

It seemed to go on forever, the whistle of wind, the rumble of wheels. Occasionally we would slow and turn, but then we'd find some even road again to barrel away for hours. Untraceable hours away from my car, from my new job, from my mother's house. She wouldn't even know I had gone missing. Suddenly that seemed like a relief. At least she wouldn't know. It would only make her more afraid. It would only make her gloat.

I must have been dozing because the screech of brakes startled me. The long drive had calmed me into a sense of complacency, as if I could exist forever in the dark, but I knew it would end. I'd have to face him and whatever he would do to me.

The roar of metal rushing against metal assaulted my ears before white light blinded me. Before my eyes adjusted, he flipped me over. He untied my hands and my legs, sending a rush of pinpricks into my fingers and toes. A moan escaped me.

"It's okay, sunshine," he murmured, rubbing his hands over my arms briskly. "Just a few minutes and you'll be right as rain."

Gradually, the physical discomfort faded and I became aware of a new sensation: hunger. Ravenous hunger that sharpened into pain and the wonderful smell of cooling fast food. He smirked, handing over a bag. I had no dignity left. I ripped into the bag, scarfing down half the container of fries before I glanced up at him. He was watching me. There was no judgment on his face, only a kind of unnerving fascination that was somehow worse. I wasn't even worthy of his pity but some curious creature, something lower. I bent my head and polished off my fries and burger and washed it all down with the soda he produced.

My body felt a little more solid now, but my emotional state frayed. He was even more handsome in the morning light, like someone I would have had a crush on but never would have had the guts to approach. It twisted me inside because as sick as it was, I wanted him to like me. I was still desperate for a friend. I started to cry.

He pulled me into his arms, curled on his lap. I held myself rigid for only a minute—small rebellions—before sinking into his warmth. He smelled of musk and spice, and I turned my face into him, letting my tears soak his shirt, clinging to him as if he could save me even while his arms held me captive.

I cried for having stayed with my mother too long, not knowing what a normal life would have been like. I cried for finally summoning the strength to leave, only to have all my worst fears prove true. Most of all, I cried because I felt relief to have been captured.

The outside world was terrifying, but here inside this large tin box on wheels, none of that could touch me. Only he could touch me. Even as I sobbed in his arms, I felt his erection harden beneath me. He made no move to use it on me, not yet, but I had no doubts that he would. That was my purpose here.

Eventually, I quieted, sniffling every so often. I may have even drowsed that way, still affected by whatever drug he had given me.

"It's okay." he said, his lips pressed against the crown

of my head. "You're so pretty when you cry."

I felt myself blush even as my stomach turned over. But I couldn't hate myself for the small pleasure I took. There were so few pleasures in life, and even less in the back of this truck, but I could accept his compliments. I could accept his pleasure too.

There were some men you didn't say no to.

I wriggled my body experimentally. I told myself it was only to test my limits, but maybe there was a part of me that wanted to seduce him. It was sick, but I wanted him to touch me more, to hold me tighter. I wanted the intimacy from last night in the absence of any true connections in the whole wide world.

I didn't know him at all, but he had touched the deepest part of me and in my own way, I had touched the deepest part of him too. There was a strange but addictive magic to sex. It tied a thin string from his soul to mine with every joining, and I wondered how many times it would take before we were inseparable. They were fanciful thoughts, but I felt that way—like dreaming, like lightness. He would bring me back down. He would ground me.

Scooting aside, I placed my hand on him, *there*. The denim was stiff against my palm, no give at all. I paused, glancing up at him.

Surprise was in his eyes, and lust too. "Go on, sunshine. You want to see what I look like? How I'm made?

Take it out."

Carefully, I unzipped his jeans and opened the flaps. He wore nothing underneath, and he fell heavily into my palm, thick and long. The skin was silky smooth against my palm. I closed my fingers around it, and it jumped.

"That's right," he praised. "Touch my cock. Stroke it for me, baby. Make it good and hard so I can fuck you with it."

It was so wrong, but I let it happen. So dirty, and it washed over me. If I went into a sort of trance, he couldn't really hurt me. It even felt good. Wasn't that better than pain? Than fear? My mother had lived in fear, and she was safe—but she was still afraid. I was the opposite of safe here, but I didn't have to be afraid. Maybe that was the ultimate freedom.

I tightened my fingers around his length and tugged. His *cock*. That was the word he used. Tentatively, I slipped my hand down and then up again.

He groaned. "More. Again."

I stroked him until his hips bucked into my hands, and I found a sort of power there. In bringing him pleasure, I empowered myself. I could wield it in the withholding of pleasure, hesitating before the next stroke to hear him beg. A small rebellion, like syrup for my pancakes.

"Get on the bed." His voice came out gutturally.

I lay down on my back, my legs slightly parted. Together enough to hide me from sight, but the small space between them was a message—I wouldn't say no to him. But he didn't climb between them, not yet. He knelt astride my body, a knee on either side, his cock resting thickly in the valley between my breasts.

He rolled my nipples between his fingers, setting off sparks that I felt down to my core. Harder, he pinched. I whimpered in response, but that made him tighten further. Only when my hips bucked up of their own accord did he release me. He pushed my breasts together, wrapping the pliant flesh around his cock.

With slow glides, he thrust between them. It should have done nothing for me. They were just breasts, and he wasn't even stimulating them really. He was just using them for his own pleasure. But the sight of the dark head of his cock excited me as it peeked from between my pale skin.

The feel of the dampness in the crevice as his tip leaked his seed. The sound of his pants above me, growing harsher, more ragged. Heat gathered in my sex, and with nothing to assuage it, my legs fell open, begging without words, without thought.

He noticed, glancing back with his cock still trapped between my breasts. "Goddamn," he breathed. "You are too perfect. I can't let you go."

It almost broke the spell, that reference to how I'd come to be here in the back of this truck. Almost, but I held onto the trance, to the cloud of arousal that made this all okay.

"Please," I whispered. "Help me."

"Yeah. Oh yeah."

He sounded incredulous, and why shouldn't he? How many captives would have been willing participants in this? How many captives had he had? But I had learned early on to make the best of my situation, to flourish even under hothouse lights, within glass walls.

"You're so good, pet," he said, climbing down my body. My legs were already open to him, already damp. He bent his head, pressing a kiss to the top of my mound. "This is your treat."

With unaccountable tenderness, he licked me, first around the soft lips, and that was shocking enough, but then he slipped his tongue into the damp crevice and swirled higher to the tight bundle of nerves. My legs shook where he had hooked them over his shoulders. I cried out, but he didn't relent, didn't let up until another blinding light overtook me, this one painful too, but also wonderful. There was no air in that place, no thought or fear in the pleasure, only his tongue and my skin and the shudders that racked my body.

He turned me over so that my face and breasts and belly pressed against the musty mattress. I waited for him to enter me from behind, as he had done last night. Instead, I felt him rustle behind me, heard the quiet snick of plastic. Coolness shocked the heated skin of my bottom as his fingers rubbed a sort of gel. But not where I thought it would go. He was putting it there, on a hole I never imagined could be violated.

I let out a soft cry of protest.

A light slap hit my thigh. "Quiet now. Just relax and it will be fine."

But I couldn't. I tensed against the invasion. It felt like stretching, like burning, and I knew it would only get worse. "Please."

He bent his mouth to my knee, speaking softly. "Am I shocking you?"

"I didn't know—"

"Well, now you do, sunshine. And you know what else? I think you're more adventurous than you let on. You've been sheltered, that much is clear. Well, you're going to expand your horizons with me."

I sobbed against the coarse blanket, feeling pinned but also freed. There was nothing I could do in this position, no way to get free.

"You need a good cry," he said thoughtfully. "Yes, I think so."

I wished he were more certain. I liked his aggression better than his twisted consideration. I wanted him to hurt me, not help me.

"Do it already." I balled my hands into fists. "Just do what you're going to do."

He froze for a minute. I felt his surprise. Then he chuckled softly. "You are perfect, aren't you? It's like you were made just for me." He shifted, pressing the blunt head against my puckered skin. "Don't tense or you might tear yourself up."

His words grated on me. I might tear myself up, as if this were my doing, as if I'd asked for any of this. Oh God, had I? Had I secretly longed for a cage to replace the one I'd left? Something inside me whispered *yes*. He was right about me being made just for him. I was an animal bred in captivity, unprepared for the harshness of the wild.

Pressure built behind me as he forced himself farther. I knew he'd only just started but it felt like far too much, like he'd split me open, like he was pressing the butt of a baseball bat inside me. I squirmed, fearful and impatient all at once. I wished he would do it quickly, ripped off like a band-aid—shove it in. But then I'd tear, and he cared enough about me to prevent that. That hurt worst of all, that small bit of respect. It showed he could feel compassion if he wanted to. It showed me how little I really had from him.

It burned, drawing out shuddering sighs and rasping sobs from my throat. With a burst of pressure that brought tears to my eyes, he pushed his way inside and sank in with a deep, satisfied groan.

"Oh, sweetheart," he said. "Oh, sunshine."

He sounded strangled, hoarse with the pleasure he took from my body. Beneath the physical sensation, I heard the gratitude in his voice, the awe, and I felt a perverse camaraderie over that. Weren't we both so surprised, weren't we both a little shell-shocked to find ourselves in the middle of a felony sex act in the back of an eighteen-wheeler in the middle of nowhere?

This hadn't been on the calendar. *Appease kidnapper with butt sex* hadn't been on my life plan, but then I'd never really had a plan. That had been the point. I had wanted to wander, to flit, and I'd flown right into a spider's web.

His hand slipped around between my legs, searching and probing until his fingers lit upon the tight nub that made me buck my hips and groan. It did more than ease the pain, it swung it around and upside down, turned it into a razor-sharp pleasure. I rutted against his fingers, seeking relief in the form of ecstasy—they came together, a package deal.

I felt a little nauseous too. My body was overwhelmed, and it wanted to lose whatever was in my stomach. I shuddered, forcing myself to swallow the muted bile, as my body was wrenched forward and back, impaled and fondled, used and taken in ways I had barely ever imagined, hardly ever thought of except in my room when the blanket of night shielded even my thoughts. I would touch myself exactly this way, face-down on the bed with my hand underneath, rocking my hips until my mouth became dry and my toes curled up tight and my mind exploded into white-hot bliss.

I cried out, lost in the heat of it, the all-encompassing pain of it as my stretched skin contracted and pulsated around his cock.

"Yes, that's right," he muttered thickly. "Milk me. Use me. Take it all."

A sudden warmth bathed my insides, the salt stinging the raw flesh. I shuddered at the pain of it, the price of my own pleasure. He rested his weight on me, and I absorbed his contented sigh with my body, cradled him as best I could while facing away. At length, he pulled free.

He gently rubbed the abused skin in the crevice of my ass. Slow strokes, tender strokes.

"Feel better?" he asked.

I would have expected that to make it worse. It had already been pummeled. This would be like pressing on a bruise. But his touch was sure and knowing, and some of the tension eased.

"Yes. How did you know?"

My speech came out slurred, and only then did I realize how tired I was. Strange, since I had slept for so long. It was a stupid question, too. Of course he had done this before, had sex with women, some willing, some not. He was only taking care of me because he wanted to use me again, putting away his toys so he could play again in the morning.

Everything seemed fuzzier, softer. He'd drugged my drink again, I realized, but I couldn't summon up the will to care. Here in this place there was no pain or fear, and the whole idea seemed just grand. Yes, keep me and play with me. Do the things I never would have the courage to do on my own and keep me safe in the process.

"Because it always helped me," he said in a low voice.

It took me a minute to realize he was answering my question. This had been done to him. Had he liked it? Who'd done it? But the questions were too heavy on my tongue, and I drifted away to sleep. The last thought before I lost consciousness was to wonder if he had been willing.

CHAPTER SIX

The longest vertical drop is over 165 feet.

THE NEXT TIME I woke up, my head was much clearer. Unfortunately, my body was coming apart. I felt every bump and rattle of the truck from my pounding headache to the rumble of my stomach. But that only fueled my determination.

What was happening to me? This needy girl, desperate to please with sex and obedience—that wasn't me. I wanted freedom, but freedom wasn't worth much if I let other people take it away with a snap of their fingers, with a passive-aggressive threat or a pill dropped into a soda. I had escaped once before, from my mother's house, and I would do it again.

This would be even easier because I didn't care about Hunter. It would be nothing at all to hurt him and get away. So as we bounced in an uneasy rhythm along some unseen highway, I tried to gather some strength into my tired limbs, some awareness into my dark-dampened mind.

When he opened the back of the truck, I staggered

out. It was so bright. So…much. Even the air on my skin felt overwhelming. Only a small amount of time kept away from it had weakened me. I scanned the treeline, looking for an escape route. His hand clamped onto my shoulder.

"Not so fast, sunshine. You stay with me."

True to his word, he led me into the bushes. We stopped at a patch of grass, and I understood this was where I should do my business.

I raised my eyebrows at him in a tacit plea for privacy.

His face was implacable. *No.*

Miserable, humiliated, I squatted down and sent a warm stream of liquid into the earth. He handed me a wipe from his pocket. After cleaning myself, I clutched it awkwardly.

"You can leave it on the ground. Those are biodegradable."

Oh great, an eco-conscious kidnapper. I tossed the wipe against the base of a tree and then realized his hand had left my shoulder at some point. We weren't touching at all, and suddenly, the air between seemed like a question—*will you run?* I stood still, indecisive. I knew I wouldn't get away like this. I could never run fast enough or fight him off. It was a question of obedience.

"You surprised me yesterday, being such a good girl," he said, grabbing my wrist. "Don't stop now."

For a minute, I was distracted from his words. Yesterday? It seemed like only hours had passed. I was losing time here. That was somehow scarier than anything he had done to me. I had lost enough time trapped in my mother's house. I couldn't afford to give away any more. I hoped he wouldn't drug me again. It occurred to me that he might not, if he thought I wouldn't run. That was when I registered what he had said about being pleased with me. And he hadn't led me to the back of the truck, but to the cab.

I stumbled out of the leaves-strewn ground, allowing myself to be tugged toward the road. Suddenly he stopped, and I ran right into his side. He yanked at my wrist, pulling me behind him.

Startled, I peeked around him to see a large cat with black and orange stripes.

A very large cat.

"Is that…?"

"A tiger. Yeah."

Though the size was abnormal for a regular housecat, it was the eyes that were different. Both more beautiful and colder. Crueler. A predator who was considering her attack. On the one hand, it seemed silly to worry over an animal physically smaller than us. On the other hand, I felt her ferocity in her stare, her stance, and I had no doubt she could cause either one of us considerable damage if she wanted to attack.

She hadn't moved a single paw since we'd arrived in her clearing. Only her whiskers twitched, gathering data from the wind.

I whispered. "Should we—"

"We're just going to walk real slow around her. She won't attack unless she feels threatened."

"Right, but—"

"Just move. Nice and easy."

We shuffled around her. In a shocking act of chivalry, Hunter was careful to always stay between the cat and my body.

When we'd made it to the other side, I quickened my step and snapped a twig. The cat's ears flicked. She lowered her head.

"Easy," he said sharply. Then softer, "Go easy. Nice and slow all the way back."

We shuffled in a sort of dance back into the rest stop where the truck was parked, continuing to move slowly and keep facing the woods until we reached the cab.

He opened the passenger door, and instead of waiting for me to climb in the tall steps, practically threw me inside. He circled the truck and got in.

"Shit," he said.

I swallowed. "She was gorgeous."

"Yeah. Good thing I didn't have to kill her."

My face scrunched up. "Could you have? I mean, if she had attacked?"

"A tiger's pretty vicious when they want to be, even a little undergrown thing like that one. But a gun is better."

I gasped, eyeing him up and down. "Where?"

"My boot. Don't leave home without it."

"So wait. Why didn't you get it out then? We could have died."

"Nah, probably not. She'd have launched herself, I'd have blocked, and she'd have caught my arm. It would've got torn up pretty bad, but that's it. She was too malnourished to do much. That's why she's so close to a rest stop. Must be near to starving to chance it."

I tried to calm myself though inside I felt shivery, bordering on hysterical. "Okay. Here's a question. Why was there a tiger in the woods? In *Texas*."

"There's more tigers in Texas than in India. The old travelling circuses let them loose when they disbanded, and since then they've maintained a steady population." He reached back and rustled in some bags behind the seats. "Most people think they're large cats. I've seen them before but never that close."

He tossed big slabs of jerky packaged in shrink wrap onto my lap.

"Open those up."

Without a word, I tugged at the little slit in the corner and pulled out the savory meat.

He drove up to where we'd reenter the freeway but

rolled a little ways onto the grass. He hit the button and rolled down the window.

"Throw it out there. Far as you can."

I stared at him for a minute, but he just waited. Sighing, I turned and tossed one of the pieces of meat onto the grass.

His exhalation was derisive. "That as far as you can get it?"

I scowled at him, then reached back and threw the next piece. It landed a few feet farther. I unlatched the seatbelt so I could turn my whole body. The rest of the pieces landed only a few feet from the treeline.

The meat rested there, small pockets of brown amid the grass.

I glanced back. "Will she find it?"

He chuckled. "Oh, she'll find it. She's just wishing we'd get the hell out of here."

With that, he gunned the engine and we sped back onto the freeway. He used his radio to tell someone about the tiger and they messaged him back something about a wildlife rescue organization going out to set a trap.

Only as the minutes ticked away did the events fall in order for me. The way he'd protected me, yes. Even more interesting, the way he'd protected the tiger. He could have shot her and been done with her. Instead he'd risked his own life for hers, he'd fed her, he'd sent help for her.

And maybe most shocking of all: I was riding up front.

He glanced over, seeming to follow my train of thought. "Cat got your tongue?"

"Are you going to make me go back there?"

After a moment, he shook his head. "Good girls get to ride up front."

The words were humiliating but stirred something inside me. I was beginning to recognize that tension as lust. Dirty, wrong, but undeniable. It was spacious in here. The seats were a soft black leather. Like the waitress had said, very comfortable.

I huddled against the door, staring straight ahead. My exhilaration from the encounter with the tiger morphed into excitement. I was in the truck! Inside the truck. I didn't want to mess this up. And maybe I would have been excited even without the kidnapping. This was like an adventure. A slightly perverted adventure of questionable consent, but beggars like me couldn't be choosers.

As the truck rumbled forward, I noticed the swaying of a necklace roped around the rearview mirror. No. I looked closer and realized it was a rosary. Pale cream beads and a silver cross. I wondered if it had belonged to someone he loved, like maybe his mother. It humanized him a little bit. There must have been someone he loved, before he had turned into this, a man who had to force women into staying with him.

We drove for several minutes in silence. I stared out the window, watching the farmland rush by. The sky was a brilliant green-blue like I imagined the sea would look, though I had never been. I blinked up at the clouds that seemed to hang above us, even as we sped eighty miles per hour down the highway, even as the clouds themselves must be floating along in a different direction.

On Earth, it was much more dismal. The farmland was brown and flat. Even someone as clueless as I knew that was a bad sign in terms of producing crops. And there were no houses, no people. Not that I could jump out of a moving vehicle even if I saw someone. We were so high off the ground, almost flying, with a tint strong enough that no one would see me wave for help.

I had traded one prison for another, this one mobile but absolute. Inescapable even as it sliced through the countryside. Neither my mother's home nor this eighteen-wheeler were gilded, but I preferred the view in this cage.

Except to the left of me, where Hunter sat, tapping the wide steering wheel in a restless beat. His legs were long, reaching leisurely to the floor. His whole body was slouched slightly, clearly quite comfortable. In contrast, my own knees were pressed together, my fists balled together right on top.

"So tell me about yourself, sunshine."

Tell him...about me? He couldn't really care, and I couldn't really want to tell him—could I? Sadly, I wasn't so sure. I had spent most of my twenty years with one person. Here was a new one. The novelty was too much to resist.

"I'm not sure what there is to tell. I'm not...anyone special."

His insouciant expression slipped slightly as he looked at me. "How about you let me judge that? Tell me what you do. You in college?"

He kept that gaze trained on me, even though we were hurtling over the road. Nervous, I glanced ahead. We were still in the lane, still steady, and he seemed unconcerned.

"Um, not anymore. I graduated...but just with an associate's degree. In graphic design."

"Oh yeah, you an artist?"

"No, it was just something good to do from home, because..." Because I was a loser who had listened to my mother for far too long. And I had stopped listening at the one moment I should have heeded her safety advice. I couldn't seem to win.

I stared at the rushing pavement as it slid under the truck. "But I was moving out. I was going to Little Rock, Arkansas. I had a job there at a camera shop."

My voice had lilted up at the end in a small challenge. We both knew why I was no longer on my way to Little Rock. I didn't even know where we were anymore, but I wasn't on track to Niagara because of him. Bringing it up had almost been an accusation, the closest I could come to things better left unsaid: *Why did you take me? When will you let me go? How could you do this to me when I had finally broken free?*

Terrified of his anger or retribution to my impertinence, I slid my gaze over to him. He didn't look mad, just thoughtful.

"A camera shop, huh? You ever been there before?"

"No."

"You know anyone who works there?"

"No."

"You like cameras?"

Despite my fears, a small smile played at my lips. I liked scenery and majesty. I liked angles and lighting. I liked seeing in a photo what I yearned to see for real. I wanted to take a picture of Niagara Falls.

"Yeah," I said. "I like cameras."

"Yours looks pretty fancy. Heavy, too."

My eyebrows snapped up. Had he looked through my stuff back at the hotel? Of course he had. And he must have been disappointed to find less than a hundred bucks. What did he think of my book?

"Where are we going?" I asked.

"Got no destination."

I blinked. I had expected him to have some delivery or route or something. Wasn't that the point of an eighteen-wheeler, to transport things?

He chuckled. "I like to drive. Sometimes I do jobs, but in between them, I keep driving."

It seemed…well, inefficient. It also seemed wonderful, like a ball without friction, with nothing to slow it down, just rolling around, seeing everything in every direction but not having to participate. Not really being able to join in, always separate.

How lonely that must be. Almost as lonely as I had been, locked up in my mother's house. That was when I realized—if this was a cage, then he was caged too. Even though he could go wherever he wanted, he couldn't escape these steel walls. My mother was trapped too, even if it was by her own fears.

Maybe we were all held captive by something.

"What's wrong?" he asked.

"I was just thinking…" I paused, wondering if it was wise to speak so openly with him. He didn't seem to get angry with me when I did, but it could be I exposed myself this way, made myself weaker by my own speculation. "I was thinking it seemed a little lonely."

He was quiet so long I thought he wouldn't answer. Then he said, "Sometimes we do things only because they are better than the alternative."

"The lesser of two evils?"

He grinned. "Exactly."

And I thought, *what could have been so bad to make him avoid all human contact?*

He was not so unlike my mother, and that thought should have made me hate him, but instead just made me sad.

"It's not as bad as all that," he continued. "I know a lot of people. People who live along some of the main lines. I'll stop by for dinner or even overnight. I know the other truckers, and I can talk to them over the radio or my cell phone, if I wanted to."

My heart beat a little faster, although I struggled to hide it. A radio? A cell phone? Methods of communication, means of escape. There was no obvious device on his dashboard, just a high-tech panel of flat screens, currently black, and buttons. Where would he keep his cell phone? His pocket? Somewhere else? Luckily he didn't seem to notice my frantic plotting.

"Besides, I have you to keep me company now."

Something about the extra emphasis on the word *company* raised the hairs on the back of my neck. He grinned, and I closed my eyes against the lust that glimmered there. But even with my eyes closed, I could feel the charge in the air, setting off little sparks against my skin, strumming awareness into body parts that had been well handled recently.

"If you're going to stay up here, you might as well

make yourself useful and keep me awake. Tell me something new about you."

"I'm sorry," I said caustically, "I haven't had a very interesting life so far. That was what I was trying to do before you—"

"Fine. What's the deal with your book? About Niagara Falls."

I didn't want to tell him what it meant to me, how it had been my goal for so long and how it tore me up inside to be battered off course.

"I can tell you a story from the book," I offered. "It's called the Maid of the Myst. A Native American myth. Have you heard it before?"

"Why would I have heard it before?"

"Right. Well, the people used to listen to the thunder, and it would teach them about the world, how to grow food and be kind to each other. But then they stopped listening, and the god of thunder grew angry and went to live under the waterfalls."

"So he just left them. Kind of immature for a god, huh?"

I ignored him. "The people suffered and they decided to sacrifice this girl, but she ran away. She takes a canoe down the river, but the rapids take over and she can't control it. As the boat fell over the waterfall, the god of thunder caught her in his arms and saved her."

"Very romantic."

"Yes, it *was* romantic. They fell in love and lived together underneath the falls."

"Hmm. Happily ever after, just like that?"

"Well, not exactly. She wanted to see her home one last time, so she convinced the god to let her go. There she realized how much she missed it so she decided to stay. In his anger, the god of thunder destroyed his home, flooding it with water from the falls."

"Anger issues. He's really not much of a catch, is he?"

"Back with her people, the girl realized how much she had changed and could no longer live among them. So she returned to the god of thunder. Since their home under the falls was destroyed, he carried them up to the sky where they watched over their people."

"And you believe this bullshit?"

Anger simmered inside me. "Why are you doing this?"

The words immediately meant more than his antagonism over the story. They were about taking me, keeping me. About hurting me when he could have simply walked away. Part of me wanted the truth, however cruel, while the other part hoped that my words had been swallowed by the hum of the motor, the quiet rush of the air outside the window.

"I don't know," he muttered.

Not much of an answer, but the raw honesty I heard in his voice felt like an opening, a crack in the veneer.

Not that he would let me go with apologies or anything that extreme just because he'd displayed a moment of doubt, but that I could learn something about this man who held me, see around the thumb that pinned me down, see beyond the walls that always penned me in. What made someone like him tick? Why did he do something like this? Had this moral ambiguity always been inside him or was it learned, evolved—forced upon him just as it was me?

"Who gave you that?" I asked softly, gesturing to the beads swaying from the mirror.

He scowled. "A man who will no longer speak my name. Does that make you happy?"

"What did you do before you became a truck driver?"

He looked at me sharply. "Why would you ask me that?"

"I'm curious," I said defensively, though not really giving up ground—not yet. "It doesn't matter, right? It doesn't matter what I know. I can't do anything to you."

"No, you can't do anything to me, not a goddamn thing. You think you're clever, huh? You want me to open up to you, and then what? Maybe I'll fall in love with you? Maybe I'll let you go? Not gonna happen. You're mine. I caught you, and I'm not giving you back."

My throat stung, but I refused to back down. Maybe I was goading him. Would it be so bad if he snapped?

Then it would be over. The words tumbled forth, unruly and vehement along the dashboard.

"You can keep my body and you can hurt me and have sex with me, but you'll never really know me. You'll never really *have* me, just like she didn't." It became a prayer, one for each bead on the rosary. "Never, never, never."

A low growl seemed to emanate from his chest. "I don't give a shit about knowing you. I just want to use you."

His hand tangled in my hair, dragging me down to the floorboards. Tears flooded my eyes at the pain—at the defeat. He unzipped his jeans and shoved inside my mouth, still guiding my movements with his fist in my hair. I didn't have time to consider whether I'd fight. I was already doing it. Not really sucking, but then I didn't have to, couldn't keep up anyway. There was salt and heat and liquid-coated skin, and then I was gagging, choking on it, hearing him tell me he still didn't care as long as he got what he wanted. He was inflamed, and I had made him that way.

"You're just like them anyway," he grunted. "Just like them, just like them."

Like a prayer of his own.

The body will cope with what it is given—that was what I learned then. My mind shut off in increments, until he hit the back of my throat and I didn't feel like throwing up anymore. I didn't feel anything at all, just floating in a sort of trance while he pulled the truck off on an abandoned weighing station. Not even when he pushed me back and I sprawled back onto the floor-board. Not even when he pulled up my skirt. I tensed slightly, braced against the impact of his invasion, but that was only physical—it didn't mean anything. He couldn't move me.

Until he bent his head between my legs. At first there was nothing. What was he doing? Then I felt it, small wet caresses. Not blinding pleasure or searing pain but slow licks, sensual caresses, and a little bit of unwelcome comfort. It felt like an apology, as he knelt between my knees. Like atonement.

The blissful paralysis I'd been floating in began to thaw with each wistful swipe of his tongue until I was making little urgent sounds and rocking my hips up to meet him and hating myself, just hating that he could draw me out so easily, disprove my grand denials. He wouldn't know me? He already did.

He saw into every corner and every secret. He gave me exactly the right touch or word that I needed to submit. There wasn't anything left to hold back, and he knew that too. His hands tightened on my ass, spreading me apart, pushing me up into his face.

He lifted long enough to say, "Come on, sunshine. Give it to me."

And I was helpless to resist, too weak to fight the mounting pleasure, too relieved to find myself spread and held and *wanted*, oh finally, someone did want me, and even if it was perverted and dirty, at least it was new. My stomach tightened first, clenching as I bucked up, seeking more. Then it spread, the tension. White-hot pleasure slid up my spine. My mouth fell open but no sounds came out. Nothing but half-cut gasps and raw groans.

Before I could catch my breath, he slid inside me. His way was easier this time than before, a smooth glide from first entry, and he took full advantage, moving at a brisk pace. He pumped into me quickly, harshly, but I didn't get the feeling that he sought his pleasure this way.

Instead, he seemed to be making a point, saying with thrusts what he couldn't put into words and cementing the ones he had. *You're mine. Try to understand, I have to do this. I'm as trapped as you are, can't you see?* Although it could have been wishful thinking, wanting to believe that the man lodged inside me, pulsing and shuddering his way through release, wasn't a monster.

He collapsed, breathing hard. His weight bore down on me, though not unpleasantly. There was safety in bondage, that much I knew. He turned his head and kissed my temple, the wisp of sweat above his lip mingling with the dampness of my skin.

"You make it bearable," he murmured, though his

voice was slurred, so I couldn't be sure. So I lay there, feeling his chest push into mine and then mine push back into his. We breathed together, we held each other. There was no acrimony in that moment, no pleasure either. Just a ship pulled into port.

Chapter Seven

The first tightrope walker to cross the Niagara Falls did so in 1859.

W E EXISTED LIKE nomads in the following weeks. We used deserted truck stops for bathroom breaks and daily showers. At night we slept in the fold-out bed in his truck. He would fuck me every night, sometimes tenderly, other times rough and urgent—though each time felt more like intimacy and less like coercion.

The hardest part was meals, because where there was food, there were people. We had a somewhat painstaking routine where he would stop a few miles out, put me in the back of the truck, then pull into a diner or restaurant and get take-out. I always debated banging on the walls, but I would never know if anyone was there. Hunter could be standing right outside and punish me for it.

Instead, I would press my ear to the metal, straining to hear anything. If I had heard voices or thought there were people, I would have beaten the door for all I was worth. Instead there was almost complete silence— probably he parked far away from everyone else—and then eventually, the steady crunch of gravel as he returned with food.

We were going through mountains now. The highways were cut into them, sliced straight through like a butcher knife, leaving a tall, straight wall of striated rock. I watched the lines bleed together through the window as the truck rushed past.

My stomach grumbled.

He glanced over. "You hungry?"

I lifted my shoulder in a shrug. He turned back to the road, but I watched him scanning the blue highway signs as we passed each exit, looking for something decent to eat but sparse enough not to be crowded.

"What's the deal with the book?"

I glanced at him. "What?"

"You told me the story from it, about the girl and the canoe. Is that why you keep it?"

I played at the hem of my dress, distracted and jittery. "Not really."

"So what's the big deal with Niagara Fucking Falls?"

Despite myself, I rolled my eyes. Leave it to Hunter to be irreverent whenever possible. "No big deal, okay? I'm just curious. Am I not allowed to be curious?"

He eyed me. "Mouthy, huh?"

I was mouthy, though I wasn't sure where the hint of attitude had come from. Was I becoming more comfortable with him? Was I coming to trust him?

Scary thought.

"So you want to go there. Then why were you heading to Little Rock?"

"Didn't have enough money," I mumbled. Then stronger, "But I guess you know that, seeing as you already looked through my stuff."

He snorted. "Okay, so why haven't you gone there before this?"

Because of my mother, I wanted to cry. But that was a lie.

"Too scared, I guess," I mumbled. It wasn't as if I had any pride with him anyway.

His gaze softened.

A smile turned my lips. "Don't imagine you have much experience with that."

He squinted into the distance. "Depends on what you're scared of. Me, I'm scared of standing still."

My heart skipped a beat at his confession. Maybe we could open up to each other after all...and then what? What as the end goal? Even Niagara had lost some of its appeal, just another point on the map, a way-station to a true and unimaginable destination.

I expected us to stop at another fast food restaurant or a diner. But this time, we didn't pull off the road for him to stash me in the back. Instead we exited the freeway where a large sign had the icons for gas, food, and lodging, and continued on until we were pulling into a truck stop.

He wasn't hiding me.

This truck stop was a lot like the first one, and it made my heart speed up. Maybe it was foolish to hope, but he could let me go here. I'd served my usefulness. I had pried into his life. I had opened up about my hopes and dreams. For whatever reason, he could be finished with me, and now he'd leave me here in a place where he found me.

So why did I feel disappointment?

It was premature, I knew, but a spark of hope could conflagrate a wildfire. If I were freed, I would call the cops, file a report, and return to my car. Then I would drive to Little Rock, where hopefully the job was still available, the one at the camera shop where I had never been. I swallowed thickly. So why did it feel like a step backward?

Faced with the loss of him, I suddenly wanted what Hunter could show me. For all that he was a little unhinged, he saw things—really saw them. I wanted that. Maybe I even wanted him to keep me.

But that was insane. Completely loco. I wasn't so far gone that I couldn't see the craziness of that wish—the same way a Kamikaze pilot must have felt in the second after he volunteered, like *what did I get myself into?*

Besides, the part of me that could be spontaneous and risk-taking had atrophied long ago. I was like my mother, bound by fear, but instead of being restricted by geography I was restrained by societal conventions. He was a bad guy, a kidnapper, and I shouldn't want anything he had to offer—not even freedom.

So I pressed my lips together and ignored the flutter in my belly. Even when he pulled into one of the long diagonal parking spots meant for trucks—right next to another one!—I didn't say anything. He wasn't even trying to hide our presence here. It was all out there in the open, in the waning late afternoon light.

He turned to me. "Don't give me any trouble, okay? Let's just have a quiet dinner."

I blinked. We would eat...and then he would turn me loose?

"If you can't be good for your own sake, do it for theirs. Anyone you get to help you answers to me, and they'll live to regret it. Understand?"

"You're not letting me go?"

He stared impassively for a moment, then he laughed. "I thought we went over this. No."

Was that relief? Oh Jesus, it was. I was as crazy as he was.

"I just thought...you might..."

His voice lowered. "Sunshine, if you're trying to look less appealing to me, it's not working."

My heart thumped in response, and I felt my eyes widen. "But the people inside. They'll see."

"They'll see that you're mine and if they're smart, they won't lay a finger on you."

I had been up-close-and-personal with this man's *cajones* and not even realized how huge they must be. He had no fear, none. He was going to walk into a non-empty place of business during the day with a captive in tow. And judging by the disturbingly self-aware smile that played at the corner of his lips, he wouldn't even break a sweat doing so.

It was strangely attractive. My own lips pursed in restraint, but I wanted to smile too, without fully understanding the humor. We could laugh at the people we would see, blind to the egregious crime happening in front of them, or maybe we'd chuckle at his chutzpah. But I feared that the joke was really on me. Stupid, naïve girl who's too afraid to cry for help in a public place. I'd show him. Hopefully.

This diner was similar in feel to the last one, both grungy and aging poorly, but this one had at least tried to be homey once. Cherry wood paneling lined the walls and formed booths over brick-colored linoleum. Fake ivy along the walls was coated in thick layers of dust. A young black waitress poured coffee at a table where three men sat.

We walked inside hand-in-hand, so I knew that his hands weren't sweating. Mine were, though, and clammy, trembling, as if I were the one doing something wrong instead of him. Hunter didn't wait for the waitress to look up. He just tugged me over to a booth.

He gestured me inside in what could have been mistaken for a courtly gesture. I scooted in and he sat beside me, hemming me in. As the waitress walked over to us, he pushed up my skirt, slipped his hand over my thigh, and slid his fingers into the crevice between my legs. I tensed.

If the waitress noticed, she didn't show it. After a quick glance at Hunter's face then mine, she turned to her notepad. "Can I take your order?"

"We'll have steak and eggs. Medium rare. Two over easy. I'll have a Coke."

He turned to me. "What do you want to drink?"

"I…I…" My lips were numb, tongue tied in knots. I could barely function on my own but now there was pressure. What if I messed up, and this girl got in trouble? She was about my age. What if he took her too? Of course, all these thoughts swirling around were making me mess up, and I sat there with my mouth open like an idiot, until she looked up from her pad.

"Orange juice," I said weakly.

After she left, I glanced over at the men, but they were engrossed in their meals. Hunter's thumb brushed over my skin—back and forth, and it sparked something very near there. I felt my skin almost ripple beneath his, as if it could urge him closer to that heat.

Abruptly, he stood and slid into the seat opposite me. "There," he said. "Now we can talk."

The air beside me felt uncommonly cool, my thigh bare. I missed his presence, I realized with dismay. He sent me a vague smile that said he knew exactly what I felt.

"Prison," he said succinctly. "That's what I did before I started trucking."

My lips parted in shock. I mean, sure, it shouldn't have been a surprise. But it was.

He grinned briefly, running his finger along a crack in the table. Then his expression turned serious…troubled. "Predictable, really. The ex-con driving a semi, preying on innocent young women. I'm a stereotype."

I frowned, perpetually unnerved by his penchant for plain-speaking. It would have been easier to take if he had sex with me in a moment of lust-madness, then walked away with the forgetfulness of the unkind. But he seemed to know exactly what he was doing with me, and though sometimes it seemed to bother him, he had no plans to stop. He wasn't lacking in morals, he was willfully going against his morals just to have me, which was terrifying but also sent a small thrill down my spine.

"I suppose you'll be even more scared of me now."

I was quiet a moment. "That depends. What were you in prison for?"

Surprise flashed in his eyes at my boldness, and good, it was time I returned the favor.

"What do you think?" he asked softly. "It's not so hard to figure out."

My throat seemed to swell, and thickly, I swallowed. "I don't know."

"Come now." His voice was faintly mocking, but who—who was the target? The answer was made clear with his next words. "I know sometimes I come across the perfect gentleman, but surely you can think of something I might do wrong, something cruel and vicious and inhumane? Say the words, sunshine."

I shook my head, nostrils flaring as my body prepared for flight, even as my mind knew there was nowhere to go.

"Aggravated rape."

The air seemed to leak from between the yellow-brown blinds on the windows, through the smudged panes of the door, anywhere but here. I couldn't breathe.

"Did you do it?"

He shrugged. "Some people thought I was innocent. The ones who counted didn't."

I thought of the rosary hanging from his rear-view mirror, of the man who would no longer speak his name. Someone close enough to gift Hunter with faith but who didn't have faith in him.

"And you." His mouth twisted in a cruel imitation of

a smile. "More than anyone, you know how guilty I am."

I found my voice. "And those girls. They know too."

"Do they? I'll take your word for it."

I shut my eyes at his cavalier tone. Didn't he care about them? Sometimes it seemed to pain him when he hurt me. Maybe it was a sickness, an impulse he couldn't control or a personality shift that took over him at those times. But he seemed fully aware every time he had taken me. I was just making excuses for the man who held my fate in his hands. False hope that he would do right by me in the end.

The waitress returned with our food, setting it down in front of a silent Hunter and myself.

She kept her gaze trained on the table. "Can I get you anything else?"

He reached into his back pocket and she flinched. But he only pulled out a handful of bills.

"This should cover it," he said. "Keep the change. And don't come back to the table."

She snatched the money and scurried back to the kitchen.

Hunter stood without touching his food. He seemed agitated after his confession, far more affected than he wanted to appear.

"We won't be stopping again until morning, so eat up. Come straight outside when you're done." He sent me a dark look. "Don't make any trouble, sunshine."

I watched him leave the diner, his confession still roiled through my body. Sometimes it was better not to know. Did he also feel sick to his stomach? Is that why he left without eating? I didn't know. I shouldn't care about him anyway.

I looked down at my food as the grease cooled, leaving an unappetizing sheen. He probably wouldn't know if I didn't eat it, but I considered it anyway, just to be obedient and to stave off the hunger for the rest of the night. But why was I thinking like this?

He'd left me—unattended.

Sure, I could see his silhouette through the musty curtains right out front. He was blocking the exit, but not the only one. There must be another one out back that the employees used. Here was my chance to get away.

Maybe I could fool myself into going along with him. Consent and cooperate and let myself be used just so I didn't have to be a victim. But that was all veneer, like the slick coating of grease that formed on my steak and eggs. It changed how it looked, not what it was.

A convicted rapist. I had no choice but to run.

I stood quickly, heading toward the back where the waitress had been. The raucous conversation grew abruptly quiet. I could feel the men's gazes on me, but I resolutely kept my eyes averted, mimicking the waitress. She'd seemed to inherently understand the dangers of Hunter and the other men. Maybe that had been my problem from the first. I'd seen Hunter leaning against the cab of his truck. I should have run in the other direction but I hadn't...and somehow that had led me here.

Like stepping through a white trash looking glass, I had ended up in a different truck stop. I'd become a different girl. One who knew how to suck a cock, for one thing. One who knew what the sunset looked like from the tallest hill as far as the eye could see. One with enough courage to run when the opportunity presented itself.

In the back, the girl was washing dishes in a large steel basin.

Her eyes flashed with fear when she saw me. "You can't come back here."

"Please. Help me. I need help."

"Not me." She shook her head as if I were threatening her. "I can't help you."

"Just call the police. Let me call them."

A large, heavy-set man came out of the back, his yellow-stained wife-beater pulling up short of covering the dark, bulbous skin of his belly.

"What's going on in here?"

The girl shook her head, tears glistening in her eyes.

"Please, that man out there, he kidnapped me. You have to call the police."

His eyes seemed too large for his head, not out of surprise, just naturally that way. I could see the whites even as he frowned. "I don't have to do anything."

I drew in a shaky breath. "He's...he's going to hurt me if you don't help."

A flash of sympathy lit his bloodshot eyes. Then it was gone.

"If I were to go calling the cops on my customers, I would be out of business in a week. Or wind up dead on my office floor."

Desperation streaked through me. I ran away from his cold, pitying stare and pushed through the back door. There was nothing but empty fields to my right. On the other side, a short row of trucks. I needed to make a decision. Hunter was still out front. His truck was out there too. Soon he'd come looking for me. I had to make a decision.

Since the fields were wide open, he'd see me in a minute. He'd catch me and what? Punish me? I didn't know, but there was no turning back now. I almost wished I hadn't run now that I saw how pathetic my options were, but it was too late for regrets.

A click from the door behind me warned me that it was going to open. I didn't know who it was, but I ran toward the row of trucks. Footsteps pounded behind me, barely audible above the rasping of my own breath. I reached the first truck and darted behind it, but I was slower than I'd hoped, weakened by days of inactivity and sparse diet. A fist tangled in my hair. I felt myself yanked back against a tall, unyielding body.

CHAPTER EIGHT

An estimated 5,000 bodies have been found at the foot of the falls since 1850.

"LOOKIE WHAT I found," the man holding me said.

Not Hunter. Suddenly my fear was a hundred times worse. I hadn't known I trusted Hunter but faced with another trucker, I knew I did. Whether it was a sickness or some sort of Stockholm Syndrome, I believed that Hunter wouldn't truly harm me, but this man?

No.

I fought in a wild clash of soft punches and hopelessness. I heard laughing and a curse when I caught something soft beneath my fingernail. Thick fingers grabbed my arms, wrenching them above my head as I was twisted to the ground.

"Let me go." It felt like a whisper, low and grating the walls of my throat, but through the melee, they heard me.

"Now why would I do that when the fun's only started?"

"He'll make you pay," I said, and knew then that it

was true.

The men just laughed.

One of them knelt between my thighs, unbuckling his belt. I closed my eyes against the sight of his thin, glistening erection. Rough hands yanked at my hem, pulling it up. The air felt cool against my heated skin before they grabbed my nipples and twisted.

Something slick poked around my thighs, sliding through the folds of my sex. He was trying to find his way inside. It felt like being violated with a fish. I was going to vomit, and the way they were holding me down, I would probably choke on it.

An unholy sound rent the air, sending chills along my exposed skin. It sounded like death. Was it me? But no, I was still on the ground. It was the man between my legs who had moved. Pain shot through my limbs as I curled in on myself, rolling to my side though one person still held my arm.

There was a shout, and the hand holding down my right arm was lifted. I flailed, hitting and scratching, though it didn't move them. Dimly, I registered the sounds of flesh on flesh—not mine though.

The sound of flesh hitting flesh was punctuated by grunts. My vision cleared. Hunter was poised over one of the guys at his feet, raining down blows onto a man. As I watched in horror, the man twitched and then laid still, his face already too bloody to be recognizable.

Hunter looked like some kind of avenging angel, but an angel would never pull a knife from his shoe with a glint in his eye. I closed my eyes, not wanting to see what happened next. I heard it instead, just the whisper of sound as sharp metal sliced through the air, its abrupt quieting as it met some solid object, and the thud of a body as it was dropped.

The final man was pulled off me, practically lifted into the air above me before being thrown a few feet in a spray of gravel. The man fought back, but he was no match for Hunter, who pummeled him until his head fell with a thud.

I sat there, open-mouthed with shock, my body still lewdly exposed. Hunter came to stand over me, breathing hard, his face a grotesque mask of violence. His hands were covered in blood and bruises. Not an angel—a demon, and somehow sweeter that a beast so savage had saved me.

"I told you not to start trouble," he ground out, his broad chest heaving.

Tears slid down his throat. Would he hurt me now? If he hit me like he'd just beaten them, I'd die. In fact, I thought for a minute that they were dead, but low groans in the air proved otherwise.

He pulled me up, keeping my dress raised and running his hands along my body. "Are you hurt?"

It hurt everywhere, but I was too numb to feel it—a

strange and contradictory feeling.

I shuddered beneath his hands.

He released me. "Get back to the truck. I need to clean up here."

Clean up? What did that mean? I ran around the diner. His truck gleamed in the sunlight, blinding me. If I got in the back of that truck, would he touch me again? Did I want him to?

Yes, something inside me whispered. *Wash them away, make me clean.*

Instead I ran toward the road. I couldn't see any other buildings nearby, but the hill crested just up ahead, blocking my sight to anything beyond. I was running on fumes after the interrupted meal and my fight with the men.

I glanced back. The truck sat exactly where I'd left. He must still have been cleaning up, whatever that meant. My muscles felt nebulous and insubstantial, but somehow they managed to drag me up the road.

At the top of the hill, the scene spread out before me with depressing majesty, a blank canvas of farmland and sky—not a building in sight. My feet slowed to a trod but didn't stop altogether. There was nowhere to run to.

Gravel crunched beneath my feet. Then louder as the truck rolled up beside me. A hiss as the brakes halted its motion, then the door opened.

"Get in the truck."

I glanced up at him. He didn't sound mad, even though I'd clearly disobeyed. He even looked handsome if intimidating up high in the cab, those intense eyes. Maybe the creepiest part was how unaffected he seemed after beating up grown men, almost killing them.

Maybe he had killed them. Maybe that was what cleaning up meant.

I kept walking. With a shudder, the truck rolled forward to catch up with me.

"Get in the fucking truck, Evie."

I stood still, thinking. It felt important, that moment. Even though I didn't have a choice, there was a pull toward him or away. At some point those men should have walked away from me—from him. But they didn't and they'd lost. Was that me? Fighting a fight I couldn't win, only to get bloodied from my efforts?

Though if I imagined myself the loser, the one wielding the punches was just life, just fear. If I looked at it from just the right angle, it seemed like Hunter could be my defense. He'd certainly figured out how to combat the inevitable.

Swallowing hard, I walked to the back, waiting for him to open the heavy back door. I just knew he'd put me back there as punishment, and I wanted it. I wanted to crawl onto the thin mattress and sob.

Instead he opened the passenger side door to the cab and gestured me inside.

With my arms wrapped tightly around my middle, I walked to the front. Climbing inside exposed all sorts of new hurts in places that had been too blank with shock. I shivered in the seat, feeling cold and dirty and alone. Worst of all and completely irrational, the hurt of betrayal panged in my gut. As if he should have protected me from them. From myself.

He got in the driver's side and started the truck without looking at me. We'd gone fifteen minutes before the tears began falling in earnest. Another five before broken cries tore from my chest, unstoppable. I hated him for not putting me in the back, where he wouldn't bear witness to my pain.

He pulled over and shut off the engine, magnifying the gasping sobs I couldn't hold in.

"Are you hurt?" he asked hoarsely. "Do you need to go to a hospital?"

"As if you would take me," I spat.

"Do you need a doctor?"

A doctor? Sure, I needed a psychiatrist. I'd probably need daily sessions for the next ten years just to make sense of everything that had happened to me with Hunter, then another ten years for everything that had happened before.

I shook my head tightly. A hospital wouldn't help anything. I didn't even care about getting away anymore. It was all a big joke, freedom. Trapped at home or trapped out in the world. Would it help to get strapped to a hospital bed? Not at all.

The sobs threatened to tear me apart. I wasn't sure how much longer I could go on this way. I wasn't sure I'd ever stop. I wrapped my arms around my waist as if holding myself in.

A muscle ticked in his jaw. "I'm sorry I...I'm sorry I let them touch you. I should have been there. Should have known you'd try to run."

A cry hitched in my throat. He'd caught onto the same perverse responsibility that I had, the implication that he should protect me even while we both knew he could hurt me.

Incredulity had a calming effect. "Don't you see how messed up this is?"

No, I didn't need to be afraid anymore. The worst had already happened—almost happened. And the truth had become clear when those men were on top of me.

I trusted him.

So I rephrased the question. "Don't you see how *fucked up* this is? That you beat up those guys for...for..." Here my courage deserted me. "For what you did," I finish lamely.

I saw the ripple in his throat as he swallowed. He looked less menacing in a side profile. Or maybe that was just the grief in his eyes. It didn't look new. It looked ancient, as if it had always been there. In fact, I thought it had been, and I'd been too wrapped up in my own sadness to notice his.

"So what do you want?" he asked. "You want me to let you go?"

I said nothing.

He gestured angrily out my window. "So leave. Get the fuck out."

Tears sprang in my eyes. Wasn't this what I wanted? Okay, in my fantasies I was dropped off closer to civilization. But even barring that, I wasn't sure I could get by without him. I hated the helplessness, but in this moment, with my flesh still warm from cruel hands, I hated even more the thought of wandering.

What was the point? Niagara Falls wasn't a person. It was just another place to be alone.

He sighed. "Let me keep you a little bit longer. You can take some time to recover. Then we can talk about what to do next."

"Are you giving me a choice to leave?"

He frowned. No, he wasn't. "I'm just asking you not to fight me anymore. Don't run from me. And in return I'll show you new places. I'll even let you sit up front."

He said the last wryly, and I puffed a laugh.

"I guess I don't have a choice."

"You do. More than you realize. But I want to…I want to keep you a little longer. I'll make it good for you. Okay?"

God, he was so messed up. This was his way of asking for a relationship.

And I was so messed up too.

"Okay."

CHAPTER NINE

The Niagara River flows at approximately 35 miles per hour.

"**W**HERE ARE WE going?" I asked, climbing down from the truck.

He grinned, a mischievous twinkle in his eyes. "Wait and see, sunshine."

Hunter had pulled off a wide dirt road. Parking was always a challenge anyplace but a truck stop, so we stopped in some grass. It was surely illegal but no one seemed to be around. We were in the middle of nowhere, and the thought occurred to me that he could dump my body easily.

But I wasn't afraid.

He was just too...cheerful, almost. Brimming with anticipation to show me something. Like a kid.

Silly thought.

We hiked along a trail and reached a tall metal marker: *Enchanted Falls, 1 mile.*

I froze, mouth open. "We're going to see waterfalls?"

He suddenly seemed bashful. "Figured since we were

passing through."

Squealing, I threw my arms around his neck. He caught me with a small *oomph* of surprise but after a second, he pulled me to him in a bear hug. It had only been on impulse, but he embraced me as tightly as if he'd been waiting just for this, as if it meant something when it couldn't.

I backed up, blushing. He cleared his throat and ducked his head, so that despite his foot and a half on me, I was looking at his profile from the top of his head. His hair was curly, I realized in the yellow-bright sun. It was cut short, but light reflected blond strands pulled through the darker brown.

He seemed more human in the light—less sinister. I imagined him in some innocuous setting. We could have met on a trail like this, just two people enjoying the beautiful setting, the smell of pine and gentle sound of water in the distance.

"It's not too far," he said gruffly.

We continued along the path. It wasn't too uneven which was a good thing, considering my shoes were basically ballet flats. I felt the shape of each pebble and twig beneath my feet almost as if I were barefoot, although less sharply. The path turned rockier as we approached, the sound rising to a roar in my ears before it even came into view.

Eager, I quickened my pace. The trail continued at

its full width forward, but I heard the waterfall to my right. I began to round a small bend obscured by the trees when Hunter yanked me back.

"Careful," he warned.

Curious, I cocked my head then turned back to the path. We crept forward together, and I understood his warning. The trail ended on a bluff overlooking the waterfall. We weren't at the bottom of the waterfall but at the top.

My heart squeezed at the sight. Water streamed down in rushes too fast for the eye to process. Mist rose up like tendrils of steam, the wetness kissing my face as I stood there.

A tall wooden fence, rotting, was all that separated us from a downward hill that met up with the shore far below.

"Can we get to the bottom?"

"Eventually."

He continued along the main path, and I followed him. We came out upon a wide river—the source of the falls, I realized. Though the water ran swiftly, it was clear and peaceful, nothing like the thunderous violence of the falls.

Looking at the lands untouched by man, I imagined a time when people might have traveled this river without a map. What a shock it must have been to anyone traveling this river without knowing about the falls up ahead.

To my surprise, Hunter took off his shoes and waded into the river.

He turned back, a grin on his face. "Come in."

"What? No."

"It's a little chilly but you'll get used to it."

"I don't do rivers. Or...nature." That was mostly because I'd never been around rivers...or nature, but I wasn't about to tell him that. No doubt he'd mock me.

"You don't do rivers, but you want to see Niagara Falls."

"I wasn't planning on swimming in it."

He made a skeptical sound. "Yeah, because they wouldn't let you anyway. This is better."

I shook my head. "Freezing to death. Falling to my death. No, thank you."

"I wouldn't let anything happen to you."

"Oh good, because I trust you completely."

At that, he laughed. "Just try it out. Nothing ventured, nothing gained."

I scowled. "What are you, a motivational speaker?"

"In another life, yes. Come on. If you don't like it, you can get back out."

Oh fine. I toed off my shoes beside his on the dry, sandy bank. The first touch of water sent a shock up my spine, and I gasped. But I forced myself all the way inside, both fearful and excited of the strange feeling of cool water threading between my toes. The current was much stronger than it looked from the surface. It felt like it was pulling me along with it, and I had to fight just to stand still. The rocks beneath my feet were smooth and slippery.

Exhilarated, I stood in the middle of the river and looked around at the trees and fog-frosted mountains. I'd seen all of this before from just ten feet away on the bank, but it was different here. Now I was immersed, experiencing the sights as well as seeing them.

A smile of wonder crept over my face. Hunter grinned back at me, suddenly looking boyish.

"Well?" he asked.

"Not bad."

"Hah. You love it."

"Okay, I hate you five percent less."

He rolled his eyes and turned to walk in the direction of the current. "Come on, let's go."

"Wait, where are you going?"

"I thought you wanted to see the waterfall."

"Uh, yeah. See it. Not fall to my death in it."

"You're not going to die."

"I know, because I'm not going over there."

He shrugged. "Suit yourself. I'll meet you back at the truck."

"No, wait. Okay, I'm coming."

I followed him through the river, feeling nervous but

excited. I was walking through a river in a secluded park toward a waterfall. I was *doing this*. And I never would have done so without Hunter. I put that thought aside and focused on my steps. I slipped off a particularly rounded rock, and Hunter reached back to steady me.

"You good?" he asked, breathless. His eyes shone with excitement too. I'd never seen him so alive, so intense except when we had sex. In a way these were both carnal things, to roam and to fuck. He was a carnal man, one who found pleasure in doing and living and being. It radiated from him, and I absorbed his enthusiasm by osmosis.

No more attitude, I told myself. Not today. *Just enjoy this.*

"I'm good," I said, grinning.

When we reached the edge, I looked down at the rush in awe. I couldn't see the bottom, just the white, glittery mist a few feet down. But farther along I could see the river continue, calm again. I felt powerful, as if the water running past my shins were channeled through me.

"Crazy," I said, not taking my eyes off the panoramic view.

"Crazy," he agreed. "And now we jump."

My heart sank. "I thought you were joking about that."

"I never joke about extreme sports," he said solemnly.

That tugged a smile out of me. I wished he weren't so endearing when he wasn't terrorizing me. I looked down at the waterfall again. Not *that* far. Definitely the kind of thing someone could survive—just not me.

"Evie," he said in a cajoling tone. "It's amazing. Trust me."

"I don't trust you," I said automatically, knowing it to be a lie.

"It feels like flying."

"Not very well, I guess, since you fall."

"Yeah, but first you soar."

Just enjoy this. "I can't swim."

He was surprised. "Not at all?"

"I have some vague memories of swimming at the Y as a kid. Nothing recent."

"Well, I'm glad you told me that before I pushed you."

My eyes widened. "You're not serious."

He shrugged. Damn, he had a good poker face. I couldn't tell if he'd been joking.

"Look," he said. "You don't have to do it if you don't want to, but it'd be fun. I think you'd like it."

His straightforward words cut through the fear that held me back. Yes, it would be fun. Yes, I'd like it. This was exactly the kind of thing I'd wanted to do but never had the means or the courage to actually do. Now, with

Hunter, anything was possible.

"Let's do this," I said, feeling terrified and wondrous. "Count of three?"

He thought for a second. "Let me go down first. It'll be easier for me to help you if you need me to if I'm not also under water."

"Okay. Right." God, this was crazy. *I* was crazy.

"Just hold your breath before you go under, and then kick your way to the top. I'll take it from there."

I nodded, unable to speak.

He leaned forward, almost there.

"Wait."

He looked back. "Cold feet?"

"No, just…is this legal?"

He laughed. "Fuck no."

Then he jumped, sending a shout that echoed through the trees around us. He disappeared into the mist, and then I heard a splash directly beneath us. A few seconds later, his head emerged farther away from the falls, hair darkened by the water and glistening.

"Come on, sunshine." The words were indistinct, but I could read them on his lips.

Oh shit. No, no, no. What if I died? What if we were caught? Which a stupid thing to worry about, all things considered, but my good-girl tendencies had been well drilled into me.

But the thing that decided me was that I couldn't *not*

do it. I couldn't walk away from this challenge, from this chance to finally live.

To soar.

I jumped.

I understood what he'd meant about flying. It felt like the air caught me and lifted me even as I drew ever closer to the shore. My vision was suffused with white spray, as if I were bursting through a cloud. The water came up impossibly fast and yet slow enough to watch with wonder. I sucked in a breath and plunged under water. For a second, I panicked—*can't breathe, can't move*. But then I righted myself and found my bearings. A few strong kicks carried me to the surface.

Hunter was right there waiting for me. He must have swum closer to me while I'd fallen. He grabbed me to him, laughing.

"You did it, sunshine. I'm so proud of you."

I wiped the water from my eyes, laughing too. "You didn't think I would."

"Nope, not even a little. You proved me wrong, though."

I looked around, awareness returning to me. "We're…"

"Underneath the falls," he confirmed.

I wasn't sure where exactly I'd fallen—maybe directly in the stream—but he'd drifted us behind the falls. There was a large cavern here between the curtain of water and the rockface that held them up. A steady stream of water pattered on my face, loose spray from the falls.

I became aware of his body, too. The weight of him, the heft as he supported me in the water. The hands that clasped my waist. Neither of us had removed our clothing and though my light sundress was comfortable enough for swimming, he was wearing jeans and a T-shirt.

"You're a little bit crazy, you know that?"

He grinned. "Just a little? I'll have to work harder."

His words tumbled into place in my mind, solving a riddle I already understood. He wanted to be this way, crazy and mean and awful. But he wasn't really. It was a struggle for him as much as I had struggled to be a good little girl in that house. A role we had to fill to keep someone else happy, except what made him think he should be this way? Someone, somewhere had forged Hunter in fire and although it didn't absolve him of his sins, I was more than ever curious about who.

Droplets hung on his eyelashes, on the coarse, stubble-covered skin of his face.

Just enjoy this.

I leaned forward and kissed him—right on his nose. A little silly maybe, but he didn't laugh. He looked startled first, then his eyes darkened. He held me still, steadily kicking to keep us afloat. But he made no move to pull away or to initiate another kiss. Just holding steady for my exploration, if I wished to continue, and I did.

His eyelids, his forehead, the rough cheeks and much softer lips. I stayed there, sending small kisses along his mouth, from one corner to the other and then back again. It was a thank you for bringing me here, for convincing me to do this. More than that, the jump had given me permission to do this thing I'd wanted, to kiss a beautiful man who held me. One who seemed to want me but was unable to express it except in the harshest of ways.

"What next?" I whispered, expecting him to do something obscene and maybe painful. For the first time, I thought I'd welcome it. It was crazy, but so was this.

His lips curved knowingly, as if he guessed the direction of my thoughts.

He raised his eyebrow. "Wanna jump again?"

And I did. We jumped five more times until we were both exhausted from the swimming and the climb. Still in our wet clothes, we sprawled out under a tree at the base of the waterfall, letting the steady hum of it lull us into a half-sleep.

"One question," he murmured. "I see them in your eyes all the time. I'll answer one question."

A million sprang to mind. *What made you this way? When will you let me go?* But one stood out.

"How many others?" I asked.

Beside me, he tensed.

Minutes passed and lengthened. I might have drifted off and then returned.

Finally he said, "You were the first. The only one."

I sat up. "What about your conviction?"

"You asked me once if I did it. I didn't." He shrugged where he lay, eyes on the sky. "Believe me or not. It's your choice."

I had no reason to believe him, and we both knew it. A court of law had found him guilty. And I knew how he'd been with me, so it stood to reason he could have done this to another girl—countless girls. Sometimes that bothered me more than what he'd done to me. I really had nowhere better to be. I was already broken in countless ways. And after today? I felt a strange and twisted kind of gratitude for what he'd done. But to imagine another girl made helpless turned my stomach.

And he said it had never happened. I was the first. I was the only.

I believed him.

He laughed, so bitterly that goose bumps raised on my chilled skin. "I told myself I was getting what I'd already paid for. They locked me up for it, so I might as well do the crime, right?"

I was silent.

He spoke in a raw kind of horror, like a man desperate, a man divided. "But the truth was, I just wanted you. I saw you looking at the sunrise, and I wanted to have that. To have you. So I took you. I knew full well how wrong it was, and I did it anyway. And the most fucked up part about it all is that I still don't regret it. No remorse. Really fucking crazy, right?"

Yeah. It was pretty crazy. And terribly sad. My heart ached for him, for me, for this crazy, messed-up world where we were enemies when we could have been friends.

"Wanna jump again?" I asked softly.

He turned to me, incredulous.

"I think I've got the hang of the landing now. We can jump together."

He answered slowly. "Yeah. I'd like that, sunshine."

Chapter Ten

Niagara is a Native American word for
"Thundering water".

A WOMAN STOOD in front of a wide porch. She was obviously pregnant, her belly rounded beneath the loose pink sundress and her hands supporting her back. A young boy rode a tricycle in circles on the gravel driveway. There were no other houses in sight, just a line of trees and then open grassy land.

The peacefulness of the scene took my breath away. It was like a living portrait, something I'd only imagined but never experienced. My heart began to pound as we pulled up close. What did it mean? What would he do?

My mind spun all kinds of horrible scenarios. Robbery and hostage situations. I silently vowed not to let him hurt the woman or her child, though I had no idea how I could accomplish that.

She didn't seem concerned that an eighteen-wheeler was pulling off the road onto the grassy area in front of her fence. *Run,* I thought. *Get yourself and your kid inside and lock the door.* But she stood there, shielding her eyes from the sun with her hand. Then she waved. Actually waved her hand in greeting though she still didn't move from her spot.

Then another idea came to me. Was she possibly…his wife? Or girlfriend? Was that his child? And as messed up as everything had been, it somehow offended me worst of all, the idea that he would bring some random girl home to his family.

Anger bubbled up inside me, warring with the helplessness. "Who are these people?" I asked.

He finished shutting off the engine. "Friends."

I narrowed my eyes. "That's not your kid?"

His eyes widened. "I don't have any kids. I wouldn't be driving around the country if I had a son waiting somewhere."

"Oh right, because you're a pillar of morality."

The words slipped out with a dry humor before I'd thought them through. He stared at me for a moment, clearly as shocked as I was. My heart beat a worried tattoo. What had I done?

He threw back his head and laughed. "Jesus. You're a troublemaker, you know that?"

"I'm really not," I said sadly.

If I had been rebellious, I never would have stayed holed up at home for so long. And I would have fought harder against him all this time. What did it say about me that I hadn't? Clearly I was too weak to stand up for myself.

Or I secretly thought I deserved it, but that was even more disturbing.

"Come on," he said. "You'll like them."

He opened his door and started to climb down from the cab.

"Wait."

He turned back.

"You aren't going to hurt them, are you?"

Something flickered in his eyes. "No. I understand you have no reason to believe me when I say that, but I'd die before I hurt my friends."

I believed him. The words settled into place inside me like a jigsaw piece. Sometimes it felt like that, like he was a puzzle and I had to search for every piece to put him back together again. He wouldn't hurt them because they were his friends—I trusted that. What would it take for me to become his friend?

Strange thought.

But I dutifully stepped down from the cab and followed him up the driveway. When we'd gotten halfway there, the little boy jumped off his trike and ran over. He hit Hunter like a rocket, right in the stomach, and Hunter stumbled back, laughing. I gaped a little, staring at the open, happy smile on his face that I'd sure as heck never seen before. They wrestled right there, while I stood off to the side, feeling oddly bereft, as if I were missing something and only just realized it.

The woman walked over to me, smiling. "Good to meet you."

I shook her hand. "Evie. Nice to meet you too."

Weird but also oddly nice. We were a couple visiting friends, two lovers on a road trip. It wasn't far off from our actual identities if I ignored the whole kidnapping bit, and as time passed, I was tempted to do just that. Maybe it wasn't even Stockholm Syndrome but simply exhaustion, resignation—sometimes it was easier to pretend.

"Hunter's never brought anyone by. You must be someone special."

That answered one question. He didn't make a habit of this. Did that mean she was right, then? If I were someone special, it was a dubious honor at best. Someone special who let people imprison her. Someone special who imprisoned herself with her fears, preferring to live through her dreams.

She continued. "We hope you'll stay a few days."

I had no idea what Hunter would do. I never did. I smiled. "I'd love to, but I'm not sure what our plans are."

"Of course." She waved it away. "I'm sure you two would rather get on your way than hang around boring married folk, but you know you're welcome as long as you want. And you feel free to ask me if you need anything. Any friend of Hunter's is a friend of ours."

What I needed was an escape plan, but I doubted she would be amenable to that considering her devotion to Hunter. And I found myself strangely reticent to tell her otherwise, to say that the man tossing a baseball with her little boy was a monster.

The screen door squeaked, and I looked back to see a middle-aged man emerge. He wore a sweater vest and a friendly smile. Hunter stopped playing long enough to shake hands and formally introduce me.

They were Laura and James Truluck with their little boy, Billy. They'd lived in this house for the past six years, but they seemed to know Hunter from before then. I was introduced as simply Evie, and I knew they assumed I was Hunter's girlfriend. The way he curved his hand around my waist and held me to his side seemed to endorse that. The worst part was I didn't even want to pull away.

CHAPTER ELEVEN

Around 40 people are killed each year when they go over the falls—most of which are suicides.

W E WENT INSIDE, where the men broke off to watch a football game in the basement while Billy played with trains. I offered to help Laura with dinner, especially now that we'd added to her load.

She set me up with the ingredients for a large, colorful salad and I went to work chopping vegetables, a mixture of store-bought and ones grown in their backyard. As she cooked the steaks and prepared garlic bread, she chatted about Billy, about the renovations they were doing on the house.

She sent me a guilty look. "I'm just talking your ears off, aren't I? It's not often we have visitors here. It's good to talk to another woman."

"Not at all." I smiled. "I don't...I haven't gotten out much, so this is nice for me too."

"You know," she said, a smile playing at her lips. "I'm so glad you're here. I know I said that already, but I...I can just see how happy you make him."

I kept my gaze on the carrot I was grating. "I don't know about that."

"Oh, it's right there in his face, the way he looks at you, the way he talks about you. I recognize that."

My throat constricted as I imagined him looking at some other woman, talking about her, even though by all accounts I shouldn't care. But maybe this would be an opportunity to learn something new about him, to gather a new puzzle piece.

"Who do you recognize it from?" I asked, and my voice came out husky.

She looked at me, surprised. "From James. When we were together, still dating. He didn't admit it was love for a while, you know men, but I knew. And I just gave him patience, you know? He came around." She laughed a little, gesturing toward the house. "As you can see."

"Oh."

Her nose scrunched. "You thought I meant some other woman? No, Hunter's never been in love before. At least, not that I've ever seen. In fact, I'm pretty sure he never expected to be." Sadness weighed down her smile, and her eyes looked into the past. "But life can take us to crazy places. I like to think things turn out for the best, you know? No matter how we got here."

"Right," I said, but my voice cracked.

Her gaze met mine, her green eyes filling with concern. "Is everything okay with you? Here I haven't given you a chance to get a word in edgewise. If something is bothering you, I'd love to lend an ear."

"No, I…" What could I say to that?

"I know men can be stubborn sometimes, always thinking they know what's right for us. It's damn annoying, that's what it is."

I gave a watery laugh. It was a little funny, that everything she said was so true…and yet hopelessly irrelevant to us. Hunter and I weren't in a real relationship.

"I don't think it's the same," I tried to offer by way of explanation. "As you and James. You seem so happy together."

"We are." Her gaze darkened with remembrance. "It wasn't always that way though. There were some bad times."

I was tempted to ask what they were. Not out of morbid curiosity. I wanted to see if they were anything like mine, either back home or with Hunter. I wanted to know if there was hope for me.

"How did you know?" I asked instead. "How did you know everything would be okay when things looked bad?"

"I didn't." She thought for a minute. "I guess at some point I found faith, in myself, in the world. Hunter helped me with that."

Hunter helped her with *faith*? Shock ran through me, but then I remembered the rosary that hung in his truck.

Was he religious at some point? Was he still? And if so, why the *hell* was he doing this? This wasn't even a puzzle piece. It was the torn off edge of one. A hint of something broken.

I opened my mouth to ask her what she meant exactly, but just then Billy ran inside. He begged for a snack from Laura who insisted he wait until dinner. James and Hunter followed. James stood behind Laura and gave her a wraparound hug that hurt my heart to see. It was like someone had taken a picture book and made it real. Exactly the opposite of my life right now or ever.

I stiffened when I felt Hunter come up behind me. He slipped his arms around my waist, mimicking James's actions. It felt like a mockery, and tears stung my eyes.

"What's wrong?" he whispered.

"Like you care," I muttered, my voice wavery.

"Don't be mad," he said, and I hated that he said that. I hated that I responded to that inside, softening a little. The truth was, I didn't like to be so full of rage and fear. It was like carrying around poison inside me, infecting me worse than the world around me. It was a relief to loosen the valve and let a little bit out. I sank back into his embrace.

His arms tightened on me. "That's my girl."

James and Billy began to set the table while Laura gently chastised them for their rough handling of the dinnerware.

I shut my eyes against the wholesome sight. "Why are you doing this?" I whispered.

I didn't expect him to answer me. He never had before. But I felt the tension that ran through him and was reminded of that jagged piece of the puzzle.

A burst of laughter pulled my attention to the family settling down at the table. Laura looked over at us, clearly happy to see us linked this way.

"How long are you planning on staying?"

The question was directed at both of us, but we all knew she was asking Hunter.

He was quiet a moment, then he said, "I'm not sure. Not too much longer, I think."

The phrasing was strange with a special weight on the words. I got the idea that he wasn't answering her but me. Why was he doing this? He wasn't sure. And the one always at the tip of my tongue: how much longer would he keep me? Not much.

Which was exactly what I wanted, so there was no reason to feel disappointed.

Laura's pretty face fell. "Oh, but you two should stop by again on your way back through."

The way back? That implied that Hunter had a home somewhere and Laura knew where it was. It implied we were going somewhere and would return. Hunter must have felt me tense, because he squeezed my hips gently.

The timer went off and Laura pulled the steaks out of the oven.

Hunter turned me in his arms. His eyes were clear in the waning afternoon light of the kitchen, and Laura had been right—he looked happier. I remembered how he'd been in the diner, mysterious but also…scary. Intimidating. And kind of sad. Laura seemed to think the change was due to me, and I couldn't really be sure. It shouldn't matter to me if it was true, but it did.

He pushed my hair from my forehead and pressed a kiss there. "Are you okay here? Do you want to leave?"

His solicitousness felt at once foreign and comfortable. He was a little crazy, swinging back and forth between cruelty and kindness, but I sensed that the former was an act, a meanness he forced on himself as much as me. This seemed natural, and I decided to embrace it for the night. Ironically, he would be himself for once, and I would be the one playing a role.

We ate dinner while James regaled us with tales of fishing with Billy at the nearby river. Apparently this house butted up against an area popular for camping and inlaid with trails.

I ended up telling them about all the places we had been. We'd ended up going through Little Rock after all, though I left out the fact that Hunter had bribed the owner of the bath house so we could have a private room in the hot springs, which was technically against the rules. I told them about digging for quartz crystals and showed them the necklace Hunter had ordered made from the pink-tinted gem I'd pulled from the earth with my own hand. I told them about rock climbing and fly fishing and then ran out of time and breath before I'd even gotten to tell them all the things we'd done.

Hunter had been very true to his word when he'd promised to show me new things.

Strangely enough, we'd come closer to my end goal. I had mapped the route enough times to know that I would probably have passed through here on my own if I had made it this far. Kind of weird that Hunter had been going the same direction. Or had he driven this way just for me? I knew he'd looked through my things, which would include the picture of the dam.

The idea that he could have done something that nice for me was too much. It expanded my chest so I couldn't breathe. It was easier to ignore the good along with the bad, and pretend we were just a regular couple on a little road trip to nowhere. A couple of wild explorers with no bond at all.

I laughed alongside them during dinner, included like we were some sort of extended family on holiday...or at least how I imagined that would be. I didn't have a large family—only my mother, and I doubted I would even see her again. Even though our relationship had eroded to almost nothing, I missed her. I especially missed her when Billy grinned at his mother and told her he loved her with his mouth full.

We finished dinner with some frosty chocolate pudding, the perfect conclusion to an idyllic day. It was made of plastic, this day, pretty to look at but an imitation nonetheless.

After dinner we cleared the table and continued quiet conversation until James whisked Billy upstairs for his bath. Laura mentioned something about fresh towels for us and disappeared, leaving Hunter and me at the table. I wondered if Laura had engineered this so we would be alone, but that didn't make much sense as we'd be alone together all night. She'd already told us which room was ours—the bedroom downstairs in the basement. One bedroom, one bed.

Hunter toyed with his mug from after-dinner coffee, apparently lost in thought. I should have been nervous, wondering what would come next, but somehow I wasn't. We'd have sex tonight, probably. And it wouldn't really hurt, would it? It wasn't like Hunter could be rough with me while the family was just upstairs. It would be regular sex in a regular house…exactly what I'd always wanted and all of it made in sand, destined to melt away with the next salty wave.

"Hunter," I said.

He grunted softly, though his eyes remained fixed on an unseen destination in the distance.

"How did you meet Laura?"

His gaze met mine. Turbulent. Pained. "Why do you ask that?"

"She seems to trust you." *And I want to trust you. But how can I do that? Help me.*

"She came to me in trouble."

"What kind of trouble?"

His smile was sad but tinged with something sharper—something like hatred. "There are men out there who would hurt a woman. Emotionally. Physically. Can you believe that?"

I didn't answer. My heart thumped in my chest.

"I couldn't, at one time. Couldn't imagine what would make someone be cruel like that. It didn't seem human."

"And then?" I whispered. *What changed that you are the way you are?*

"And then I realized we aren't all human, at least not the way we were supposed to be. Sometimes our soul dies and then we're just...muscle and bone walking around, with no purpose, no morals to contain us."

I remembered the way I had felt in that motel room: only skin, no heart. Only a body, no feelings.

"What made you that way?"

Something glittered in his eyes, something that made my breath hitch in my throat. "You know, don't you?" he asked. "You know what would make a person like this. What might take away their power, their consent."

He spat the last word, as if it were vile. What was he saying, that *he* had been raped? It didn't seem possible. And yet, I knew it was true. It was as much a confession as I could ever hope to get. It was a crucial piece of the puzzle even if I couldn't yet step back and see the whole.

I wanted to cry but my eyes were dry as bone, wide and shocked. He was strength and vitality, how could someone...? How could anyone...? But they had. He'd fought off three men at the diner, but somehow one man, or maybe more than one, had overpowered him enough to do *that*. How helpless he must have felt, how worthless.

"I'm sorry."

He sucked in a breath. "You would apologize to me? After what I..."

My insides twisted at the few words of admission, the small sign of his guilt. "I let you."

"Don't fool yourself. I made you do it. You aren't responsible for any of this. I absolve you."

I absolve you. The words didn't sound as strange as they should have spoken out loud.

"Your room is ready," Laura said cheerfully, emerging from the hallway with the basement. I wondered how much of the conversation she had heard, but her eyes were guileless, her small smile genuine.

I almost wished she had heard, so someone else could

know without the pain of telling her. But she was clueless, and I was still alone.

Hunter seemed to recognize my disappointment. He smiled sadly. "You won't find friends here. At least, not ones who will stand up against me."

I LAY AWAKE, held captive by the iron-hard bands of his arms, clenched in his legs, completely imprisoned by the hot brand of Hunter's body. He overpowered me, overheated me until I sweat and wriggled uncomfortably in his embrace.

"What?" he said, slurred.

I froze and remained still for a few minutes until his breathing evened out, then I pulled gently from his arms. I made it to the edge of the bed when he caught my wrist. He tugged me back, and I slammed against the hard wall of his chest. Breath whooshed out of me.

"Where are you going?" His voice was gravelly with sleep.

"Drink of water," I managed to get out.

He released me. "Go then."

I stumbled to the bathroom and cupped the water from the faucet in my hand, sipping it, gulping it down greedily while I wondered if I'd lost my one chance to get away.

The bathroom light shut off, plunging me into darkness. My hands fell open, splashing water in the basin. I felt the air rustle behind me then his hands grabbed my hips, yanking down the underwear I'd worn to bed. I grasped the edge of the counter, expecting him to enter me from behind.

Instead he spread my legs even farther, so I could barely keep my balance except for his hands supporting my thighs. Then I felt the touch of his tongue on my sex, gently running over the outer lips and between. He suckled me and kissed me, and I understood it to be an apology in the dark, a plea for relief from the anger I harbored for him. But anger was like a flame and without fuel, it would gently peter out. I was awash in pleasure, rocking gently against his face, completely succumbed to wherever the currents would take me.

His lips found my clit, sucking me, nibbling me. He licked there insistently with the hard, insistent press of his tongue, and I cried out softly and came in small shudders, feeling wetness spill from my sex into his mouth.

When I had come, I tried to move away, but he held me in place, leaving bruises in the soft inner flesh of my thighs as he held me open for more of his mouth. The curl of his tongue, the lightest touch of his teeth. My fingers ached from holding onto the counter, but I thrust my hips madly, wildly, until I came again and a tear ran down my cheek.

He released me then, but only to pull me over to the bed. He tossed me onto the sheets like I weighed nothing, like I was nothing, and I splayed there, waiting patiently for whatever he would do. He shrugged down his jeans, and even in the dark I admired his form. Now I could only see the lean lines of his silhouette but I knew from experience how his abs were marked by the muscles there, his hips sloping inward, his body beautifully formed.

He climbed over me, straddling my face with his knees. He liked it this way, I had learned. He liked the control it gave him, and maybe now I understood better why. I could do nothing but take the broad head and thick shaft into my mouth. He controlled the depth, the angle—everything. I couldn't even move my hands, my arms trapped tightly to my sides.

He pushed into me again and again, rocking and rocking, muttering about how fucking sexy I was, how he couldn't control himself around me, how he wanted to do everything to me, everything, everything and I would let him, wouldn't I?

"Wouldn't you?" he asked me, but my mouth was full of him, and I could only mumble a muffled answer, my tongue undulating futilely against the underside of his cock while I said *yes, anything, everything.*

"You trust me, don't you?" he asked. His eyes were black in the dark light, glittering down at me. He pulled out so just the tip was in my mouth and leaned down so that his mouth was closer to my ear.

"You trust me not to break you?" he whispered.

And it was ridiculous, of course, because I couldn't trust him at all. I knew that and so did he, but I nodded, rocking the hard, pulsing flesh in my mouth as I did so. He released a small amount of precum, salty and sharp on my tongue. The taste of it made my sex clench and liquefy, because we were in tune like that. Even when our mouths spoke lies and our hearts cried out, our bodies knew how to communicate with each other.

At my acquiescence, he reached back and pushed my hands to my sex.

"Touch yourself. Make yourself come."

I rubbed the same way he had rubbed me, fingers pressed against the hard nub and pushing, frantic.

He pushed back inside my mouth, deeper this time. Slow and steady but farther in. In fact, I hadn't realized how far he could really go—that he must have been holding back all this time. He hit some barrier, and I felt my eyes widen, panicking.

"Keep fucking yourself," he muttered, and my fingers sped up.

With a grunt, he pushed deeper, popping back into my throat, and I felt my eyes roll back. It stretched and pained me, but my sex throbbed with the entry, welcoming him. I kept rubbing my clit, and it felt almost like an orgasm but instead of a few short pulses, it seemed to climb even higher.

He reached down and covered my nose, pinching gently.

"We're going to do this," he whispered, though I wasn't sure who he was talking to.

Tears streamed from my eyes and fell down the sides of my face. He was blocking all my air, with his cock, with his fingers, but the weirdest part of all was that my fingers never stopped.

Everything grew hazy and dreamlike, like the whole world going out of focus except for the sharp and blinding pleasure of my sex. I might have screamed around his cock as I came, shuddering and begging and feeling more than I had ever thought possible.

I was reborn in that moment, burst into flames like a phoenix and floating in pieces to the ground. There was scorching pain and hope for a future unknown. I felt his cock pulse in my mouth, felt the seed flow down my throat, filling me up and keeping me warm—giving me sustenance to rise up from the ashes.

He released me, pulling his erect cock from my mouth and curving his body around mine as if to protect me, but from what? *From him*, came the answer deep inside me. Tears slipped down my cheeks—no longer mine. His.

"Your story," he said hoarsely. "The book got it wrong."

"What?" My tongue was heavy in my mouth, half-drugged on euphoria.

"It's an old Native American legend but the explorers who came through changed it to make the natives seem more barbaric."

I tensed. He had known the story all along? It made me wonder what else he'd kept quiet about. His breath puffed against my neck where his face was buried.

Dread filled me. "So what really happened?"

He murmured the words so rapidly. They washed over me like rushing water.

"She wasn't running away from being a sacrifice, she was going off to kill herself. That's the girl you identified with, that you saw as yourself. She was going away to die."

Pain clenched my heart. It didn't matter, some story that had been told and retold hundreds of years ago. It had nothing to do with me and yet everything. She'd had the courage to run away, and that had bolstered me to do the same on my birthday weeks ago.

The truth was she'd given up. Whatever had happened in her life had been too heavy, and she'd sought the end over a waterfall. It made me wonder if I should have done the same.

It made me wonder if I already had.

How did he even know this story? He'd claimed not to. Or had he? I asked if he knew it, and he'd asked why he would.

Not a denial.

He presented himself as a crude, cold trucker, and it wasn't that hard to believe. But sometimes, a certain light would shine in his eyes, something intelligent and burning bright, and I was convinced he was faking it. There was nothing to say a trucker couldn't also be cunning, but in those moments, I became convinced that he was dumbing himself down to play the part.

The bigger question was why. Why did he feel the need to live this life, to be this man? What invisible shackles were on his wrists and ankles?

I swallowed. "The rest of the story was the same?"

"Almost. There are some variations on the love story, but in every Native American version, the girl returns to her people. She conveys the message of the god, and so her people are saved."

Hot tears sprang to my eyes. "And the god is alone."

His arms tightened around me.

"Yes."

I couldn't breathe within his embrace, but I wanted it anyway. Too hot, too sweaty, but I wanted his heat. I was a caterpillar, my many limbs held tight to my body, wrapped up in a cocoon. He paved the way, eased me from a small and ugly life to a beautiful one. The transition had been painful at times, but never more than it would be to leave him. But that was the path of a butterfly—to fly away from the one who had made her.

CHAPTER TWELVE

Only three people are known to have lived going over the falls without a safety device.

A FTER A TIME, Hunter moved off me. I woke staring up at the knotted oak ceiling of the basement. Anger welled up in me, making my breath come shorter. Hunter sat on the edge of the bed, elbows on his knees, head hanging low.

"You bastard," I said, breathing hard.

I hit him, right there, the back of my hand against the hard muscle of his arm, and again—my hands clenched in fists, pummeling the impenetrable shield of his body.

He let me.

He never moved to defend himself, barely moved at all except on impact from each small blow. I let loose my rage, expecting a storm and found only a light rain. I fell still, my breath heaving as I knelt on the bed.

"You're angry."

My laugh was caustic. "Damn right, I'm angry. You could have killed me."

"I wouldn't have."

"Just like you wouldn't hurt your friends, you wouldn't ever hurt a woman," I said sarcastically. "You're so fucking full of virtue that I can't even breathe."

I stared at the golden skin of his back, his arms—completely unblemished. He wasn't hurt by my blows, but maybe my words could wield more damage.

"Who hurt you?"

His shoulders tensed.

"Who bent you over and fucked you in the ass?"

"You shouldn't talk like that." His voice was deceptively mild.

"Oh, you don't like it when I use bad words, is that it? You like me innocent and compliant, right? Is that how you were when someone shoved their...their *cock* in your asshole? Did it hurt?"

"Yeah."

I blinked, surprised he had answered me. "How did he do it?"

"They. How did they get the jump on me and hold me down? That's what you want to know?"

No, not really. It sounded horrible, even if I had cause to hate him. I would never wish that on anyone, not even Hunter. Especially Hunter.

"How?" I whispered, some demon inside me, some spirit who knew he needed to tell me.

He shrugged slightly, a lift of one muscular shoulder.

"It's not that hard when a man isn't expecting it, when he's caught unaware and alone. When there's no one to help him. They were experienced, and I wasn't as tough then. I didn't need to be."

A deep breath. "Did no one hear you?"

He looked back, his gaze hard. "I didn't scream, Evie. I prayed."

I closed my eyes against the turmoil in his gaze but that only gave canvas to the horrible picture of his words. Hunter on his knees, Hunter held down, Hunter praying...for help, for mercy? It didn't matter. It made me want to throw up.

"Besides," he said as casually as if he were speaking about the weather. "It isn't muscles that make you strong. It's how much you want it. Those guys at the diner? I won that fight because they didn't want it as badly as I did. They didn't want *you* as bad as I do."

"Why?" I asked evenly. "Am I some sort of revenge against the world? Or we're all animals so who cares anyway?"

"Doesn't matter how it started. I'm not letting you go."

"But you said...in the kitchen...not much longer. You said so."

He paused, at war with himself. "You want this as much as I do."

My breath left me for a minute.

"You're delusional," I forced out. "You're telling yourself that so you feel better about what you're doing."

"Who the hell else are you going to let touch you now?" he burst out. "Even before I got to you, you were so damn tied up in knots that I can't believe you actually drove all the way out there. Now I've…"

Broken me. I remembered his question from earlier. Did I trust him not to break me? But he believed he already had. He believed I would never fight back, and maybe he was right to think so. Even if I'd had a good reason not to fight in the beginning, when I'd thought he might truly hurt me, why not now?

Strangely, I realized that he wouldn't really harm me. He'd physically restrain me from getting away, but he wouldn't kill me for trying. So what was stopping me? Unless I really did like this. Not fighting had become a choice now. If he'd ever stolen my free will, it had surfaced completely now. If I wanted to get away from him, I could.

How much did I want my freedom?

Enough to fight a man I'd come to care about? Enough to break my promise to him not to flee in exchange for the places he showed me? As wonderful as these weeks had been, I was still his prisoner. I'd been given toys for my cage, been taken on walks to sniff around, but in the end I was put away at night on the mattress in his truck where he used me for his pleasure—

and for mine.

Carefully, I scooted down in the bed and rolled over, pulling the sheet up over me. After a minute, I felt the bedsprings shift.

"That's it?" he said, and I knew I'd surprised him.

It wasn't hard to sound tired. "We can talk about it tomorrow."

He chuckled softly. "Are you shutting me out like we're an old married couple? Should I go sleep on the couch?"

I ignored him, snuggling deeper against the pillow and tugging the sheet up to my chin.

He muttered something I couldn't understand. The bed dipped, and then I heard his steady footfalls creaking the wood across the floor. He reached the small bathroom where he'd grabbed me earlier—and gone down on me.

The door closed.

A squeak and shudder as the shower turned on.

He'd already taken a shower—we both had—but he'd seemed agitated. Just like he had at the diner when he'd left me inside. His past was his vulnerability, an Achilles heel on a body otherwise flush with armor. Even thinking about it, talking about it, made him need to be alone. He left me alone.

Last time I had made a run for it and it hadn't worked out, because the people were too afraid of

Hunter and whatever retribution he might hold for them. Would James and Laura be scared of him too? No, they seemed completely unafraid, but that was because they didn't know what he'd done to me—what he was truly capable of. They had more to lose, considering Billy.

I didn't believe Hunter *would* take retribution on Billy or any of them. But it was a gamble and for once, the stakes weren't only my life.

It isn't muscles that make you strong. It's how much you want it.

I threw back the sheet and stood, glancing wildly around the room for something to knock him out...or lock him in. A couple of wooden dining room chairs were piled in the corner of the room. Out of place in a bedroom but most likely kept in the basement for storage. I hooked one under the doorknob, hoping he didn't hear the thump over the water, praying it would hold.

The shower kept running, so I tugged my dress over my head, covering my panties and tank top. My heartbeat thudded in my ears. Like before, there was a moment of doubt: was I doing the right thing? Maybe I could have reasoned with him. But like before, it was too late. I had crossed the Rubicon. I was committed.

I climbed the stairs and emerged in the darkened hallway. I crept into the living room, scanning the side tables for a phone to call the police. Nothing. Creeping along the walls, I moved toward the kitchen. Walking through the darkened doorway, I ran into a warm chest. My scream came out muffled.

"Hunter?" I breathed.

"Evie?" It was James. "Are you okay?"

"Oh God," I groaned, slumped back against the wall. The kitchen light flickered on, blinding me for a moment.

James stood there in his robe, holding a glass of water. "Are you okay?" he repeated. "I didn't mean to scare you."

I would have to tell James. I had hoped to avoid this part, even though they would certainly have found out when sirens pulled up outside their house. Maybe it was better to give him a warning. Was there etiquette for escaping from a kidnapper inside someone else's house?

My mouth opened, mute against painful, confusing words about a man I'd come to care about. God, it was true. I did care about Hunter. There were very few people in this world who had ever bothered about me, and between him and my mother, he was preferable.

Pitiful.

"I—I've been k-k-kidnapped," I said.

He stared at me. "What?"

"I've been k-kidnapped. B-by Hunter." Deep breath. "He kidnapped me two weeks ago and has been k-kkeeping me in his truck with him. I need to c-c-call the police."

He stared at me intently and then ran a hand through his hair, making it stand up at odd angles and adding a comical edge to the situation. Or maybe that was just my hysteria.

"Please tell me you're sleeping," he finally said. "This is some sort of waking dream or…something. I don't know. Jesus."

A tear fell down my cheek. "P-p-please help me."

"Okay," he said. "Just calm down a minute. We'll sort this out. Where's Hunter right now?"

"No, you c-c-can't talk to him." Panic bubbled up, not just for me but for James. I didn't really believe that Hunter would hurt these people, but I didn't want to throw the dice if I could help it. I tried to reason with him. "P-p-please, let's just c-call them. I swear I'm t-telling the truth, and if I'm not, they'll figure it out anyway. Please."

He stared at me, sorrow creeping over the bewilderment in his eyes. "You're serious."

I nodded.

"Jesus." He ran a hand through his hair again. "Okay, go ahead and sit down. I'll call the cops."

I sank into the chair while he went to the phone. He'd already dialed when Laura appeared at the door.

"What's going on?" Her eyes were wide, frightened.

Either she'd heard the tenor of our voices or just smelled the fear in the air. It was something I'd learned in my time with Hunter, that fear had a primal scent, a universal sign to get out while you still could. That was what the workers at the diner had done. *You're on your own,* they'd said, thus saving their own behinds, and I couldn't blame them. But there were people like James who didn't think twice about trying to help me when he realized I was in trouble.

People like Laura.

James kept running his hand over his face, through his hair. It was a nervous gesture on repeat.

He spoke into the phone lowly. "Yes, I have an emergency. There's a girl here. She's in trouble. It's at my house. She's been kidnapped."

Laura gasped, her gaze darting between me and James. I could almost see the switch flipping inside her, from sweet country woman to mama bear. She marched over to me.

"By us? Is that what you're telling them? Explain this to me."

"Hunter," I whispered. Dread settled in my gut. It couldn't have been that easy.

"Kidnapped," she said flatly. Then louder. "You want us to believe he *kidnapped* you, when we all saw you walk in this house of your own free will?"

"What was I supposed t-t-to d-d-do," I cried, silently

cursing my stutter. "Run d-down the road in the middle of nowhere? My c-c-car is back in the motel where he t-took me."

I hated that I couldn't explain myself better, more clearly, but I was too agitated to form the words clearly. *You could speak just fine with Hunter,* an inner voice taunted. As if I trusted him. I hated that I trusted him.

Laura pulled the phone away from a startled James and slammed down the receiver. For a moment, no one spoke, and the room was alight with the sound of our heavy, fearful breaths.

"Laura," James said softly. "If she's telling the truth…"

"No."

"We have to at least help her. If she's lying, they'll find out."

"After he's been dragged to a jail in handcuffs. Someone with a prison record. They aren't going to give him the benefit of the doubt. Are you going to be responsible for that?"

His hand ran over his face, through his hair. "If she's telling the truth…"

"She's not. Hunter would *never*—" Her voice cracked.

"Look, I have a hard time believing it too, but he never was the same after he got out. You know that. And I have no reason *not* to believe her."

We were silent. I stared at them, feeling myself tremble but curiously detached. It was always easier to let someone else decide my fate. I'd certainly had enough practice.

The phone rang.

Laura picked it up. "Hello? No, I'm sorry, that was a misunderstanding. He thought I was in trouble, but I'm fine." A few more answers and she hung up. "They're going to send a squad car by in the morning to check up on us."

James's hands finally stilled at his side. "Laura. If she's telling the truth, we have to help her."

Laura's expression hardened. "Even if I knew for sure she was telling the truth, I'm not going to help put Hunter behind bars again. No matter what."

My stomach turned over. So that was it. Once more someone had seen my helplessness and turned away. That this was more personal, an old unexplained loyalty to Hunter made it bittersweet but no less painful.

How sad, to realize my mother was right after all. Her righteousness tasted like acid in my mouth. I hadn't wanted to believe it was true. What a lonely world. So very cold.

Distantly, I heard banging coming from downstairs. Hunter was done with his shower.

I stood and walked to the back door. Laura was demanding I come back. James was asking me to give him a chance, promising he'd help me, that he was on my side if I'd just trust him. What a joke. I unlocked the door and stepped outside. The night air was cool on my face, sprinkled with early dew. Sunrise was just a strip of blue along the horizon, barely peeking from its slumber. I crossed the lawn in my bare feet, the grass tickling my soles. Then faster. They'd go down and let him out. Any second he would come barreling after me.

How badly did I want to be free?

I picked up speed, running over the ground, the darkened green blurring beneath my feet. Faster and faster, until my breath sawed through my throat, until pain stabbed my side. I went toward the line of trees. They'd talked about the lake out back where they'd gone fishing, part of an elaborate trail and camping grounds.

Brush tugged at my dress, pulling at my hair, the small pain sweeter because I knew it meant freedom. Each small rip of my skin, each bruise of a rock beneath my bare feet was the soft plunk of a coin in exchange for one more second in the wild. Like an animal, I ran with no direction, no plan, my singular goal to escape.

I ached everywhere, inside and out, but still I continued, and finally I understood fully what Hunter had meant. I thought in those moments that I would die from this alone, that my heart would burst out of my chest, that my body would seize and fall to the ground, but I kept going. It wasn't even wanting something badly, it was wanting it more than death. It was dying for something and being reborn.

Minutes, hours passed as I ran through the trees. I could run forever and not see another person, I thought. I could fall down and never get up, but more than relief I wanted freedom.

Sunlight broke through the trees, irreverent to my hopeless wandering. Birds chirped as I passed by, going about their day while I hungered and ached. Just like the people had done. I was alone, but I didn't want the statement to wring sadness from my heart anymore. I wanted to be like Hunter—content in my solitary travels. Though when I had begun to look up to my captor, I didn't know.

Adrenaline was a sweet elixir rushing through my blood, giving the world a lovely orange glow. Everything seemed breathless and yet wonderful, gasping for air and laughing all at once. It was almost as sweet as the rush of orgasm when he—no, I wouldn't think about that.

That had been wrong. Disgusting, even. He had warped me into thinking it was okay, even for a few minutes, for days, weeks. I didn't want to do that again, not ever. Which was convenient, because I couldn't imagine doing it with anyone but him.

That was only the limitation of my experience, I reminded myself. I straightened. I was going to try lots of things. Maybe not sex, but there was more to do in the world than that, wasn't there? No one would call me naïve when I was finished.

I walked for some time before my feet began to bleed. The grass had seemed like manna at first, like a magic carpet that had carried my away, but now it caked onto my sore feet, dragging me down.

I tried to think smarter, strategically. I didn't have any of the things from my backpack, didn't have my car, and I was alone in the woods. Not an auspicious beginning to my newfound freedom. But I resolved to keep going. Just keep walking and I'd find something new. Something better.

The afternoon waned into dusk, the edges of my vision tinted with purple. I could only see trees in every direction. I was so tired. Thirsty too. My worst fears began to surface in the delirium. I wasn't cut out for the regular world.

Gradually, like the drift of a cloud, I became aware of the tinkling of water. I stopped walking and cocked my head to listen, then headed in that direction. It felt like I'd never find anything, like maybe it had been a mirage even as the rush of water got louder, the taste of moisture in the air grew thicker.

Shadows lengthened on the ground and pooled into darkness. Night had fallen. I glanced back the way I had come and saw only darkness. How far had I gone? Miles, light years away. It was impossible to tell and didn't matter anyway.

I was too far away to be found by Hunter. Too far to ever find him again, even if I wanted to, and an inexplicable sadness stole my breath away.

The ground beneath my feet turned from grass to muck then to wet sand. I stumbled out onto a steep beach. Gentle waves lapped at packed sand. A burst of joy and relief pushed out of my body as a laugh. I stumbled down the bank, washing my feet in the frigid water. I splashed it on my face and drank it down.

When my feet were numb from the cold, I reluctantly returned to the shore. A soft of smoky air tickled my nose. Fire?

Running over the heavy sand, I saw a reddish point of light in the distance. The closer I got, the hazier it became, large and weighty—a campfire on the beach, and that meant people. I felt light, flying, almost there.

Two black shadows burnished with orange approached me while I babbled: *p-p-please help me, oh I'm so glad I f-found you, I was lost.* One of them got a blanket and draped it over me. Slowly the shapes turned into people. They were young, maybe my age, maybe a few years older. Both male, though I would have been hard-pressed to use the word man. Despite the scruff marring their faces, they both had a boyish quality. It was their eyes. No worry there, no hardships weighed on them. They did not seem overly concerned with my hardships either. One took a sip from a beer bottle.

The other examined me with detached curiosity. His dreadlocks were tied back with a ribbon, his shirt ripped down the side, exposing pale skin stretched over slender ribs. "Where you from, sweetheart? You damn near gave me a heart attack. You came out of nowhere, like you flew from the sky."

I blinked. What a strange thing to say. "I was running away from—never mind."

It was a relief, I told myself. These were exactly the type of people I had been seeking in the first place. They didn't take things too seriously, not even a dirty, bruised woman stumbling out of the woods. Maybe they were even thrill seekers. That would explain why they were out here in the middle of nowhere, camping on the beach. Devil may care.

The circumstances may be strange, but I wasn't going to waste this opportunity. In fact, as the seconds ticked by, instead of calming down, adrenaline flooded my system.

"I'm Evie. What're your names?"

The one with dreadlocks said, "I'm Trevor. That's Rob."

"Nice to meet you." I laughed, still a little lightheaded from the lack of food or water or sleep. "Well, T-T-Trevor, I'm going to t-tell you something. I've had a really bad d-day, but that's over now."

"Yeah, because you're here now. You can stay with us."

"Actually I probably need t-to find a town." And a police station.

I didn't relish the thought of turning him in, but I didn't have a way of getting back my stuff without him. My car, my camera—my book. Some days I wondered if the book meant more to me than the place.

"It's a hike up that way." Trevor waved down the river. "We're going back tomorrow morning if you want us to show you."

Relief flooded me. "That would be great."

Rob popped open a beer from their cooler and held it out. "Thirsty?"

✧　✧　✧

"Hold her down."

I woke up without air. Someone was on top of my chest, holding me down. Something else was clamped over my mouth, blocking my breath. I struggled, managing to dislodge the hand long enough to suck in precious lungfuls, but by the time I could focus again, my arms were bent backward, trapped in the sand by two heavy knees pressing down, cutting off circulation.

Trevor straddled my chest, mauling my breasts. My dress was pushed up, the thin fabric bunched around my neck, making me feel even more trapped. My breathing came faster. Dark spots danced in front of my eyes. I was going to black out. Maybe that would be best. Then I wouldn't have to feel what came next. But I might not wake up. Already I struggled to breathe, jerking and flailing for unblocked access to the crisp night air.

Slowly, I stilled. Around me, there was motion. The men were moving over me, around me. Hurting me. I stared up at the stars. They were so bright out here. There were never so many at home. Was this the price to see them?

A sharp pain stabbed at my center. My entire body recoiled from his penetration, writhing in the sand with nowhere to go. The night sky blurred as tears filled my eyes, and the twinkling lights melted and swirled. It reminded me of a painting I'd seen in a book, swirls of blue and yellow. Maybe the artist had cried and painted what he'd seen. Maybe he had been hurt too while looking up at the sky.

How had this happened? I'd agreed to stay the night in their camp. They were hiking back to the nearest town in the morning and they'd take me with them. Oh God, oh God. Had it been a lie to keep me there? Or I'd just been too convenient.

The world was exactly as awful as my mother had said it was, but I didn't even wish to be home. Like the girl in the story, the true story, I wanted to take a canoe onto the river, to let it slip over the waterfall and never have to worry again.

This time, Hunter wasn't here to catch me. No god of thunder to keep me safe.

I was alone, though I'd lost something precious, something important along my harrowing trip through the trees. I'd lost fear. So let me die, let me hurt. I didn't care, and the detachment lent me strength.

With a force unknown, I snapped my head forward. My forehead cracked against the man on top of me. I shoved him off me and started to get up. Other hands dragged me down, but I kicked and screamed. I bit down on fingers until I tasted blood and felt my teeth grind against bone.

Blows rained down on my head, my stomach. I fell to the ground, gasping for air but taking in sand. Pain blossomed all over my body as they closed in on me. They huddled around me and kicked, and I stared up at the sky, my body jostled about by their currents, tipping over the edge of the waterfalls and falling, tumbling to a welcomed conclusion.

A crack rang out and one of the men fell over my body. There was shuffling and shouting, then another crack and a thud beside me.

Hunter, Hunter, is that you?

Someone came to stand over me, blocking the stars. Not Hunter, I realized. Never Hunter because I'd left him. Just an ordinary man, and I understood what had sent the girl out into the canoe. *Why did you catch me from falling?* I wanted to die.

CHAPTER THIRTEEN

At the current rate of erosion, scientists predict the Niagara Falls will be gone in around 50,000 years.

I WOKE UP bound to a bed, my arms held immobile beside me, my whole body weighted down and sweating. *No, not again.* I fought, kicking and punching my way out of the restraints. A man appeared over me and held me down, shouting something I couldn't make out.

"Hunter!" I screamed his name, though I didn't know whether it was in anger or a call for help. My heart beat against my chest like a drum. God, he'd made me this way. If he was going to domesticate me, he had to damn well *keep me from running away.*

Resigned, I slumped down on the bed, sobbing quietly. I was the crazy one.

"It's okay, you're okay," a voice said.

He sounded relieved, I thought.

I opened my eyes to see an older man blink at me with worried eyes. "It's going to be okay."

With a sigh, I said, "Just do what you're going to

do."

"I'm not going to hurt you."

Oh sure, like I'd believe that. Then again, Hunter had never really lied about his intentions. That was just the warped way he saw the world.

This man didn't seem like he would hurt me. I had to doubt my ability to read people considering my lack of experience and my general state of confusion where Hunter was concerned, but I didn't feel threatened.

He was old, with wrinkles falling over rheumy gray eyes and more hair in his eyebrows than on his head. His plaid shirt was faded and worn but clean, buttoned all the way up.

"Who are you?" I croaked.

"You don't remember?"

I closed my eyes. The memories were slowly coming back, even though I didn't really want them to. Running through the woods, meeting those boys. Fighting them off.

I met his gaze. "You shot them."

He nodded. "They brought it on themselves."

I looked down and saw that the sheets had been tucked around me—not tying me down but keeping me warm. My skin was clammy. I struggled to sit, and the old man kept his distance, probably having learned his lesson after struggling with me earlier.

"You asked me not to call the police, so I brought

you back here to heal. The fever broke last night, I think."

"How long?"

He looked up, a little uncertain. "Oh, maybe three days. Sorry, not entirely sure. Time passes a little different when you're used to being alone."

Yeah, I could sympathize with that.

I finally glanced around the cabin, taking in the small bookcase with pulp thriller novels, the open shelf with blackened pots and pans, the small, ancient-looking television.

And only one bed.

He caught my line of thought. "I slept on a roll in the corner."

I'd put him out of his bed. "I'm sorry."

"Don't you worry. It was just like camping again. But now that you're awake, maybe you want to reconsider calling the police. Or at least let me take you to a hospital. They can check you out better than I can."

I shook my head. "No cops."

My heart had gone from twisted to torn right in half when I'd run from Hunter. But however much I might rage against him on the inside, I didn't want him behind bars.

Unfortunately, waking up didn't mean I was fully healed. Though I had no broken bones that we could tell, there were enough bruises that my body wanted to rest all day long. The man's name turned out to be Jeremiah, and he was generous with his space, his food, and his stories.

True to his word, he never laid a finger on me. In fact, he was exceedingly careful of my personal space in such cramped quarters. He knew what had happened to me from how he'd found me. He told me the first day I woke up that "those boys" wouldn't bother me again, and I couldn't summon enough compassion to ask if they had lived or died.

Instead Jeremiah shared with me stories of a young man in the Wyoming wilderness, tales of hunting bear and running from geese that I wasn't sure whether to believe but I enjoyed all the same.

Three days after I'd arrived, I was sitting at his kitchen table eating scrambled eggs and hotcakes for breakfast. He began telling me a story of how he and his friends had gone up to "the falls" for a buddy's bachelor party. There was something about smuggling a stripper over the Canadian border, but I had to interrupt.

"Niagara Falls?"

"One in the same, darlin'. You ever been?"

"No, but I want to."

"Oh, it'll blow you away. Right beautiful it is. 'Course nothing's as beautiful as what Candy had to show us—"

"How far away is it?"

He scratched his forehead. "About five hours or thereabouts."

My spirits sank. That was a long way away for someone with no transportation. Or money. I toyed with my eggs, but I could feel Jeremiah's curious gaze on me.

"You know," he said. "There was a time I had dreams about those falls, even if I knew they wouldn't come to nothing."

"Really?"

I figured he was just saying that to make me feel better. How many other people hung their hopes on a waterfall? But I appreciated the gesture.

"Well, if you haven't noticed, I'm a bit of a hermit. But even us hermits, we have people we look up to. Something to work toward. And ain't no hermit better than the Niagara Falls hermit."

I made a face. "You're pulling my leg."

"Nuh-uh. He was a real guy back in the eighteen hundreds. Francis something-or-other. He lived on an island right in the falls. He'd climb over some wooden planks and sit on the end like he was on a dock somewhere. People would scream, thinking he was going to fall."

Despite myself, I was intrigued. This hadn't been in my book.

"Did he fall?"

"Nope. Lived there happy as you please for years.

Then one day he was gone into a shallow portion to take a bath like he always did. Went under and never came back up. Just goes to show."

"Uh. What does it go to show?"

"Goes to show people think what they want to think. The man was highly-educated, well-traveled. Been to all these countries. Famous for his music. But he goes to live in the falls and everyone assumed he was crazy."

"But you don't think so."

"Nah, he just knew a good thing when he found it. The falls is beautiful, so why should he leave?"

I couldn't stop thinking about that man. The hermit. He knew a good thing when he found it. Was that Hunter, living isolated in his truck? Or was I trying to romanticize something so it would sit easier with me? It didn't really matter. In the end, Hunter did what he did. And like Jeremiah said, people would think what they wanted to think.

In two more days I was strong enough to go outside. I took short walks but kept close to the cabin. I'd need to leave here soon, and that meant I needed money.

I asked Jeremiah about it when he came to stand on the porch to smoke his pipe.

"I know this is a long shot, but you wouldn't know anyone around here who needs graphic design work, would you?" I sighed. "That's pretty much the only marketable skill I have."

He seemed thoughtful. "Nope, can't say that I do. I barely know what to do with those computer things, but I have one if you want to look around for a job or something."

I raised my eyebrow, doubtful. "You have a computer?"

He grinned, showing off his missing tooth in the front. "Bet you thought I was just an old stupid hillbilly, didn't you? Well, I am. But my daughter keeps trying to get me hooked into that stuff, so she got me set up. It's in the kitchen cabinet underneath the sink."

Excited, I ran to the door. On a whim, I stopped and gave him a kiss on his cheek.

"You're not old or stupid."

His eyes danced. "But I am a hillbilly."

I laughed on my way inside. "And I love you for it."

I pulled out the laptop and cables, which were pretty new as far as I could tell, and thankfully not messed up from being in a damp, enclosed space for so long. There was a little router that pulled up a signal, though it was slow all the way out in the woods.

The cursor waited patiently for me to type some search terms about a job nearby. Or maybe there would be some kind of assistance program for homeless people—which I basically was at this point. Or if I were really desperate, I could try to get in touch with my mother.

Instead I typed in Hunter's full name. Apparently there was a B-list actor of the same name so I had to scroll through a few pages of search results until I found the one I was looking for. A news site reporting on a conviction for aggravated assault.

Nineteen year old parishioner...

Spiritual advisor and close friend of the family...

Abused his position of authority...

Guilty and sentenced to five years in a medium security prison...

A priest?

Jesus Christ, Hunter had been a *priest.* No wonder Laura had been so sure of him. And yet, what I'd told her had been true. How had he come to this? Why had he done it?

I went back to the search results and found a new article dated one year later.

U.S. Federal Appeals court tossed out the conviction on Friday...

New evidence brought forward by the victim's friend...

Had fabricated the story over a series of emails...

Released on bond pending official exoneration...

The conviction was overturned.

My palms felt sweaty on the keyboard. A girl had lied about him. Lied to get attention or for whatever reasons, and he'd gone to jail for that. Where Hunter had gotten raped. The article didn't say but I knew it with a certainty bone-deep. A priest who had raped a teenage girl would be exactly the kind of person targeted for assault by the other inmates. He wouldn't have stood a chance against those men.

The first article had a picture of him. I returned and studied it.

The same features. The same man.

But the younger Hunter had a smooth face and guileless eyes whereas the Hunter I knew always wore a certain level of scruff. And his eyes were haunted. The pain he held was more marked now that I had seen him before.

Even though the picture had been taken from the shoulders up, I could see the changes in his whole body. His cheeks were more gaunt now, his shoulders broader and thicker. He'd gotten leaner while bulking up on muscle. He even held himself differently, more proud before, now defiant.

I had once wondered who had broken him, and now I knew the answer. That girl had when she lied about him. The judge and jury had when they convicted and sentenced him. His fellow priests had turned against him. The inmates had attacked him.

The whole world had turned against him and in a way, he had cracked. He wasn't entirely right in the head. Even knowing this about him, caring for him, I had to admit that his actions at that motel had been inexcusable.

But in another way, he wasn't broken. He lived, he felt, he suffered like any person.

More than other people.

A clink sounded on the kitchen table beside the laptop. Car keys.

I looked up at Jeremiah. "No way."

"Don't give me a hard time about this, missy. I know what I'm doing."

"I can't take your car."

"You take it and go where you want to go. Then if you still need a place to stay, you come back here. Ain't no use for a man as old as me to be alive if he can't help someone who needs it."

"Jeremiah. I don't have a license. If I get caught—"

He cackled. "Lord, girl. I don't have a title for that car neither. You just don't get caught."

I narrowed my eyes. "Did you steal it?"

"Grand theft auto, is that what you're trying to charge me with?" He sat down opposite me and grew serious. "About four years ago I was wandering the country, hitching rides and doing what I had to in truck stations to earn money for food, if you know what I mean."

My heart clenched. "Oh, Jeremiah."

"Now, don't go feeling sorry for me. I made my bed, and I never really regretted it neither. But this one day a guy met up with me in the stalls. We did our business and he handed me the money—along with the keys. I figured it was some kind of setup, but I took it anyway.

"Drove straight to my daughter's house even though I hadn't spoken to her in a decade. She was real good to me. Put me up for a while, helped me access my VA benefits, and I finally could afford this house. Kept the car, though. Now it's yours."

My heart felt overfull. "Okay. I'll use it but I'll bring it back."

He shook his head vehemently. "I don't need it. I'm an old man with nowhere to go. I get groceries delivered twice a month. I figure that man at the truck stop saw that I needed the car more than he did, and that's why I'm giving it to you. Just get where you need to go. That's all that matters."

CHAPTER FOURTEEN

Rainbows appear almost every day as sunlight reflects off the mist from the falls.

As I PULLED the old blue Toyota next to a parking meter a mile away from the Niagara Falls State Park entrance, it occurred to me that there may be nothing here for me.

Groups of people bustled by laden with strollers and diaper bags. Concessions were sold from street vendors. Signs announced that the Maiden of the Mist—this being the name of the ship—gave tours. Even the skyline was populated erratically with tall business buildings. It was all far more modern and commercial than any of the pictures in my book had been.

But the falls fulfilled their prophecy and took my breath away on sight. Or rather, on sighting one of them, because the expanse of the three falls together was far more than I could have visualized before. It felt enormous—and considering it divided two large countries, I supposed that made sense. There were multiple rainbows arching over the falls, closer than I'd ever seen one but also see-through…rather ghostly, really.

I went to an exhibit where I heard some of the same facts from the book, about the daredevils who went down the falls in barrels, about the tightrope walker. There was even a short segment on the Hermit of Niagara Falls, which I found gratifying in the extreme. After all, if Jeremiah hadn't been stretching the truth about that, maybe all the other stories were true too. I hoped so. It was a full life. Some good, some bad, but the man knew how to have adventures.

I did go on the large boat to get up close and personal with the falls, getting drenched despite the poncho they gave us. There was an option to go into the tunnels behind the falls, though I found cave-dwelling far less interesting without Hunter there to float with me.

By the time I had seen all there was to see, the day was waning. I counted the money Jeremiah had loaned me, feeling guilty all the while. *Get where you need to go,* he'd said. But I was here, and I still hadn't found what I was looking for. It was becoming less clear what that really was.

I fed the parking meter and walked over to the hostel that I'd found online before coming here. Thirty bucks got me a clean bed, even if I did have to share a room. The girl barely looked up from her book when I came in. I glanced at the cover and did a double take.

Everything You Wanted to Know About Niagara Falls.

"I read that," I exclaimed.

I knew I sounded like a moron, but I couldn't help it. Alone in the world, it was nice to find common ground in even the smallest ways.

"You going to work on the Maiden too?" At my puzzled look, she continued. "The Maiden of the Mist. I'm studying to pass the test so I can be one of their tour guides." She rolled her eyes. "Sorry. Adventure guides."

"No. At least, I hadn't planned to."

But there was a thought. I had most of the information memorized already. At least then I could earn back the money I'd borrowed from Jeremiah while I formulated a new plan. Still, I felt ambivalent about the falls. It wasn't their fault I'd pinned so much on them. They couldn't deliver me what I wanted, I knew that now. I'd probably always known.

The girl shut the book and groaned. "The first person to map the Niagara Falls was a French priest in 1678." She considered. "Well, except for the Native Americans. So I guess the book is wrong."

"Yeah," I said wryly. "I've heard that."

She tossed it onto the bed. "Sometimes I think history isn't really what happened. It's how you look at it."

I grinned. "You and me are going to get along fine."

"You got a name?"

"Evie. And you?"

"Sarah. I moved here with my dumbass boyfriend.

Well, I didn't think he was a dumbass at the time. But we broke up because he is, in fact, a dumbass. And a cheater. Figure I might as well make some money while I sort this shit out."

"That sucks, and I understand completely."

"Wanna grab some dinner?"

"Let's."

We left the hostel room and returned to the darkened streets. The crowd seemed to have swelled as night hovered over the earth. It appeared the locals came here for the concessions and games along the strand.

A tall Ferris wheel blinked bright in the sky. On the ground, everything felt mildly damp and chilly. It would only be worse at the top, and that decided me.

"Have you been on that?"

Sarah looked up, blinking against the mist. "Not yet, but I'm game."

We purchased our tickets and waited in line for thirty minutes before climbing in. It took another ten minutes before everyone else was loaded inside and the wheel began to turn in earnest.

"So what's your story?" she asked.

I thought about that while we circled back down to the ground.

"Kind of the same thing. Hooked up with a guy for a while. Left him. Now I'm trying to figure out what to do next."

"Asshole."

"Yeah. Except…I mean, yeah he really is. By any-one's standards, he's an asshole."

"But…"

"But nothing."

"You're in love."

"He's a jerk. If I told you everything he's done, you would totally agree."

"You haven't even told me what he's done and I already agree with you. But you love him."

"He's a priest."

That gave her pause. Then she shook her head. "Doesn't matter."

"Oh, I think that matters. Plus other stuff. It's just so frustrating. I want to go back to the way things were before I found him."

I frowned, thinking how terrified I'd been that first night. Now here I was making friends in a hostel, exploring a new place on my own. I didn't have much of a plan or much money, but neither did I have any fear.

My heart skipped a beat. No fear. That's what I'd been looking for, and I'd found it.

"Well, it doesn't matter now. I don't know where he is, so even if I wanted to find him…"

"Which you do."

"I can't."

She sighed, looking out over the purple-and-blue-hued falls. "Well, I know exactly where my boyfriend is. At our apartment with my friend. Who I only let stay with us because she needed a place."

"That sucks. Big time."

"So screw them, right?"

"Yeah."

The word sounded hollow, and judging by the look on her face, she knew it too. But she let me off the hook, and we chatted pleasantly as we grabbed a greasy hamburger from the strip and made fun of the wax statues in the window of the museum.

"I'd better head back," she said. "I've got that interview first thing in the morning."

"Sure thing. Let me just stop at my car to grab my bag."

We headed through the thinning crowds toward the hostel. I pulled the small bag of toiletries I'd packed out of the backpack. Something caught my eye. Standing in the open back door of the car, I looked up in the sky and saw an orange-ish light streaking across the sky, like a rainbow but brighter somehow.

"Look at that." I pointed.

"Oh yeah, I saw that last night. I think it's a lunar bow."

The book had mentioned those alongside rainbows but it didn't have a picture. It was beautiful, more striking than all the colors, I thought. Just one. I felt a smile spread across my face. As silly as it was, I felt like *this* was what I'd come here to see. After all the official sites, the gorgeous views, just a swash of orange across the sky. Bold, brash. Everything that I wasn't only a few weeks ago, but not anymore.

I glanced to the side.

There was a large overfill lot meant for people who visited with trailers and RVs. In that lot was a familiar truck, and leaning against the side was Hunter. I couldn't be sure. His body was nondescript from this far away, his face in the shadows. But it was him.

He didn't move. He *wouldn't* move.

I turned to Sarah. "I have something kind of crazy to tell you. I'm going to leave now, but not in my car. Do you want it?"

"Uh, what?"

"It's okay if you don't, but it just sounded earlier like you might not have one. This car is old and not even strictly street legal but it can get you where you need to go."

"Is this some kind of trick?"

"Take it or leave it."

She raised her eyebrows. "Take it."

I tossed her the keys as I headed down the trip. "Nice meeting you, Sarah. Good luck."

She raised her hand in a tentative wave. "You too."

I wanted him to come to me. It wasn't just a pride

thing. I needed to know that he wanted this too. I needed him to need me too. Sure, I suspected, I hoped, but this was put-up or shut-up time. This was putting everything on the line just to see if it stuck. It was jumping off a cliff.

The streets thinned out right away. Only the main strand had been crowded. I found the largest street that would take me to the highway and just kept walking.

Twenty minutes later I saw headlights illuminate the road beside me. I put my thumb into the air like I was hitching a ride. The familiar squeak and rumble as the truck slowed to a stop beside me.

The door opened and Hunter was there, a grave expression on his face.

"Where you headed?" he asked, deceptively calm.

"No place in particular."

"Isn't that usually the point of hitching a ride, to get somewhere?"

I grinned, repeating his previous sentiments back to him. "I like to travel. Sometimes I do jobs, but in between them, I keep travelling."

He paused, seeming to think that over.

"Well, hop in then," he said so softly I barely heard him.

I climbed into the truck and tossed my bag in the back. Without looking at me, he started up the engine and took us forward. Though I didn't have a destination in mind, I expected him to pull out onto the freeway. Instead he kept going down Main Street past the turnoff.

"Where are we going?"

He reached under his seat and handed me a book. "Got something for you."

I touched the familiar cardboard cover, traced the lettering. *Niagara Falls.*

Once the mere thought of this had sustained me, small doses of hope. Now that I'd seen the real thing, I couldn't regret any of it. The falls were both more beautiful than I could have imagined—and yet meant so much less. They were rock and water, not meant to be anyone's salvation. Not like flesh and blood.

There was more. A manila folder was tucked between the pages and sticking out from the sides. I opened it. My breath caught at what I read. A full confession written in Hunter's hand detailing how he'd kidnapped me, the sexual acts we'd performed in clinical terms, and signed by him at the bottom.

Even more shocking was the letters beneath them. Signed witness statement from Laura and James. A small pain stabbed my heart imagining Laura's horror and confusion at learning the truth. And some man named Roger Wilbourne, proprietor of a diner and gas station, who had seen a girl call for help, who'd found three unconscious men on his property later that day. Hunter had collected statements from them that were both factual and damning.

The truck slowed to a stop.

I looked out the window. The sign on the old building read Niagara Falls NY Police Department. My stomach churned with revulsion. *No.*

With an impassive expression, he nodded for me to get out of the truck. To go into the station and hand these documents over. The gesture took me back to that first day at the motel. The forced casualness, the banked desire. He'd claimed to want my body that night, but he'd really needed so much more.

This wasn't about right or wrong, love or hate. If I sent him back to jail, no matter that he was stronger now, he could get raped again.

"I would *never* send you back," I said through gritted teeth.

He stared at me, gaze burning with unnamed emotion. "What the fuck do I care if I go back? I can't keep you either way, so what do I care where I am when I'm alone?"

I shuddered from some combination of shock and want. We were standing in the water at the top of the cliff, the water rushing around us, threatening to pull us under.

"Why can't you keep me?"

His expression was incredulous. "You know what I did. How it was between us. Even if we don't tell anyone else, you know."

"I forgave you that night, remember."

He snorted, unbelieving.

"You were a *priest*. Of all people, you understand forgiveness."

Something dark flickered in his eyes, and in those shadows I remembered what he'd once told me. *I didn't scream, Evie. I prayed.* And fallen over the cliff, crashed into the water as fast and as deep as any person could do. It wasn't a surprise he'd become isolated and cold in the aftermath. It was a surprise he'd survived at all.

"Don't you see? I can't ever be normal again. Never be the kind of man who can give you a real home—"

"I had a home. For twenty years I was trapped inside one. Now I want to roam. With you."

"I'll never be the kind of man who can be gentle with you, Evie. Not like you deserve."

He was talking about sex, promising me more nights of bruising hands and forceful sex and sweaty, panting, screaming into the dark.

I met his gaze. "I'm not the kind of girl who needs gentle. You aren't the only fucked-up person here, you know."

"You shouldn't talk like that," he said mildly.

"And I was broken long before we even met."

"You're not broken." He almost snarled the words, his ferocity terrifying, compelling. "I love the way you are. The way you're terrified but do it anyway. The way you stand up to me when you shouldn't."

I climbed over to him, throwing my knee over and straddling him. His whole body tensed as if it had been shocked, rigid instead of welcoming.

"What about the way I fight for us," I whispered, "even though you're trying to push me away?"

In a rush, he grasped me to him, sucking in lungfuls of air as if he'd been underwater, his face buried in my hair. "Yes, that. God, Evie. Jesus Fucking Christ, Evie."

"You shouldn't talk like that," I teased, but then he was kissing me, consuming me, and I was falling, drowning, battered and bruised by the rapids, never wanting to surface. His hands were everywhere, fluid on my thighs, my breasts—but not stopping there, never resting, just moving over me as if making sure I was all there, as if taking inventory, possession and never letting go.

A rap on the window wrenched us apart. Outside, a police officer stood, implacable and severe.

Hunter rolled down the window.

"Everything all right in here?" The cop directed the question to me.

Hunter tensed beneath my thighs, as if I might say *no, actually, I'm being held against my will* and then hand him the signed confession.

"I'm fine."

One eyebrow raised. "You sure, ma'am?"

I blushed as my vulnerable position, splayed over

Hunter's lap, came to me. I must look ridiculous to him, helpless to him, and I was.

"Well, I am a bit embarrassed."

The cop hid a smile. "Yes, ma'am. Just making sure."

He headed back into the station.

I watched him go as a rush of exhilaration pumped through my veins. But when I turned back to Hunter, the air rushed from the space. His eyes were rimmed with red. His lips trembled.

"You honor me," he said.

I swallowed. It wasn't my fault if he went to prison, wasn't my fault if someone there hurt him. But the truth was, it wasn't mercy that kept me mute or stayed my hand.

I'd found in Hunter a kindred, broken soul. We didn't fit in with the rest of society and never really would—but neither did we deserve to be locked away or abused for our issues. We hadn't asked to be this way. All we wanted now was to live in peace.

In his own fucked up way, he'd honored me that day at the motel. He'd picked me instead of anyone, he'd plucked me out of my nothingness.

I rested my forehead against his.

"Let's go," I murmured.

His body released its tension, reveling and accepting. "Where to?"

"I have something to show you."

Chapter Fifteen

Niagara Falls Ontario Canada is known as the Honeymoon Capital of the world.

HUNTER FOUND US a hotel that had an overflow lot for his truck, and we went back to Niagara Falls the next day. We covered the same ground, the same tours, the same boat ride, and I found it all the more exciting with Hunter's sardonic presence.

As we disembarked from the Maiden, I asked the lady at the desk whether she knew of Sarah who worked there.

"She'd be new," I explained. "Just hired."

The woman shook her head. "I don't think so. But I don't run orientation, so I wouldn't really know."

I hoped Sarah had taken the car and gone home. The falls were beautiful, but I knew that any place could be a cage if you felt trapped.

Hunter surprised me by stepping forward. "Excuse me, do you have any trail maps for hiking in the national park?"

"Of course." The woman slid a glance down his

body. "I'm guessing you're looking for the more advanced trail routes."

I blinked. Was she flirting?

"You might say that. Just looking for a great view." He pulled me close.

The woman eyed his hand around my waist then grinned. "Understood. You know, if you're really hardcore, there's a whole route mapped out. They call it a self-guided tour. You hike and camp on your own but the maps will guide you as you go. It takes you all around the whirlpool and the hotspots in the park."

His eyes lit up. "That would be perfect."

Hardcore? Oh yeah, that was him.

We wove through the crowds while Hunter started ticking off all the things we'd need for the trip. I was silent—speechless, really. Astonished at the easy way he donned a solicitous manner with her. That was him, I realized. The old Hunter who had gone to seminary school and counseled families. And maybe the true Hunter still underneath all those rough, jagged edges.

I was surprised, too, that the woman didn't see what he was. I supposed he looked handsome and rugged in the waffle tee and faded jeans, with an ever-present layer of scruff on his jaw. If she sensed any of his wildness, it only gave him a more compelling edge. Something different from the dads who emerged from minivans in the parking lot around us in polos and khaki pants.

We found an outdoorsy store nearby and loaded up on new clothes and gear, trying on clothes and making faces at the ones we didn't like. Hunter snagged me in one of the dressing rooms for a kiss. As if we were a couple. The idea of us as a normal couple was...quite frankly, terrifying. But also amazing, and I suspected the two always came as a pair.

The world looked different in the park. If the gorgeous view of the falls were the front parlor, then the park was the family room—less impressive but more relaxing. It was the same thing we'd done in the smaller waterfalls where we'd stood in the water and looked down, although this place was much more expansive and these rivers were miles away from the falls themselves.

The ground we covered turned orange, the skies grew vibrant.

We walked a hundred steps carved into rock to reach the peak of a mountain, and the view had stolen my breath. Or maybe that was because the air was thinner there, but I felt rooted to the spot, indelibly planted into the ground, connected to the earth in a startling and soulful bond. This was the Niagara I had dreamed about, the true wonder that hadn't been commercialized.

Hunter was affected too. Some of the lines in his face had eased, the russet glow painting his face with wonder. But despite our auspicious beginning, he became increasingly distant as time passed. Considering Hunter was already so thoroughly contained, that was saying something.

He grew more pensive. Sadder with each passing day. The physical strain of the climbs and the harsh environment acted as buffers. It was hard for me to talk, much less convince him to open up, but with every step, it became clearer I would have to. We set up the tent and opened up the top. Sex beneath the stars, murmured conversation about the vistas or animals we'd come across, and then sleeping wrapped up in his arms. Bliss, if I wasn't sure something dark brewed beneath the surface.

Now my whole body ached with newfound activity. My throat was dry. Hunter held out the canteen without looking over. I took a gulp and returned it to his outstretched hand. He insisted on carrying the bulk of the gear.

I covered my eyes with my hand and squinted at the trail ahead. As far as the eye could see, there were shades of orange and yellow, golden rock and a blinding sunset. Far in the distance I could see heavy clouds and the slanted stripes of rain. There were a hundred different climates here, flash floods beside a desert, but it had been a full day since we'd met the river.

Dizziness distorted my vision. My foot landed on loose pebbles, and I skidded down the incline a few feet before Hunter's firm grasp caught me. He set me right again.

"You okay?" His voice was gruff, dry from the dusty air.

"Yeah, I'm good. Thanks."

He grunted and continued ahead.

His head bent low, skin beaded with sweat. The start of a beard obscured his expression, but I knew his mouth would be drawn tight, lips parched. We were both at the ends of our endurance, though his physical strength far surpassed my own.

The little safety class we'd taken warned us that people still died here every year, and though I doubted it would come to that, neither did we need a case of acute exhaustion. We wouldn't reach the basin with its shops and watered campgrounds before nightfall, which meant another night of camp.

We should bed down now so we didn't lose too much water, but Hunter seemed hell-bent on going forward, like he was trying to get away from something. Or trying to drown the darkness in exhaustion.

He shortened his strides for me, but I still struggled to keep up. Unlike some of the other straggling groups we sometimes waved to in passing, he and I stayed close, within five feet at all times. It was a safety precaution, both physical and emotional. He was my ship in a tempestuous sea. I was the talisman he kissed before a storm. Even distracted and discontent, he always kept me close.

My breath began to come in pants, my vision blurry. He rounded a corner, and relieved to hide my weakness for a moment, I leaned back against the jagged rockface. As a testament to how bad off I was, the cool prodding of rock into my back felt relaxing, massaging out some of the kinks in my muscles. Even my skin felt tight—parched.

"Evie?"

I blinked and Hunter came into focus. He looked worried.

"Hi."

"Shit," he said. "God fucking damn it, why didn't you tell me you were dehydrated?"

I frowned. "I just had a drink."

He wasn't listening though. He steered me down from the small ledge we'd been walking and onto the dirt. I let him lead me beneath a tree and lay me down on one of the sleeping bags. Sitting down beside me, he lifted my head and helped me drink.

Nausea assailed me. I pushed the bottle away.

He produced a washcloth from our pack and poured water from the canteen.

"No," I protested. "There won't be enough."

He shushed me, pressing the cloth gently on the overheated skin of my neck, cooling me down with every soft wipe. "Then I'll be thirsty."

I smiled weakly. "Sorry I'm a lightweight."

He leaned down and kissed my forehead. "It was my fault. I never should have pushed you so hard."

"I wanted to keep up."

"You will. One day soon, you'll run circles around me. It takes time to build up."

I blinked up at him in the waning light. All along, I'd thought Hunter was the hermit in the story, but as I watched him at ease against the earth, his silhouette a sleek extension of the ground and sky, I realized it had been me all along. I'd been the one cut off from society, dangling off a ledge on a waterfall just to feel alive. I wasn't used to this activity…but I would be. He would see to that, and so would I.

"How are you feeling?" he asked, concerned. "I can go ahead and bring back help."

"No, I swear I feel better."

It was true. Like a colt standing for the first time, I was wobbly. It would take time and practice before I could walk and run and gallop on my own.

"I'll rest tonight and we'll go back in the morning. And I'll be more careful from now on, let you know if you're going too fast."

At that, he smiled with remorse. "Not that I've done a great job at listening so far."

"You will," I mocked him gently. "One day soon you'll be the most sensitive guy around."

He laughed, squeezing some of the water from the

compress onto my face. I shrieked and laughed too, drinking down the drops that fell into my mouth.

He wouldn't let me help put up the tent, but that was okay. I was learning my limits, what they were and how to respect them. He needed to be kind and I needed to receive kindness.

That night he pulled back the top of the tent, and we lay in the jumble of sleeping bags and pillows staring up at the stars. I rested my face on his chest, feeling the steady rise and fall while the crinkly hair tickled my nose.

"Tell me," I said softly.

Beating beneath me was a strong heart, one that had started off pure but tainted now. Poisoned when no one had believed in him, poisoned when the men in jail had hurt him.

There was poison inside me too. Because of what had happened to me with Allen, because of the guilt from my mother. Neither of us could purge ourselves of it completely, but we could help each other. Like the way I'd read the old settlers of this place would deal with snake bites, lancing the wound and sucking out the venom.

And so the words began to flow.

"He was my mentor in seminary school. The man who gave me that rosary. Norman had already graduated but while he was working as a missionary, he'd had a crisis of faith. Some of the things he'd seen...the atrocities that men will commit on other men. On women."

My heart swelled with sadness for him—that man, but mostly for Hunter.

"We became friends though. I was starry-eyed, naïve. Idealistic in the extreme. He started off jaded, but he seemed to calm over the years I was there. Norm taught me what he knew, and he told me later it felt like he was relearning it. Neither of us questioned that it was God who had brought us together as the best of friends."

He went silent.

"What happened?" I whispered.

I already knew the way this story ended, but I wanted to hear it. And maybe he needed to tell it.

"We were lucky. When I graduated, two positions opened up in the same parish. We loved that place, the church, the community. At night we would talk over dinner, debating the same passages over again. It was…" I felt him swallow. "It was everything I had dreamed of having."

"And then?"

"There was one family there with a teenaged daughter. The parents were wealthy but both very busy. The daughter had come to our Sunday school, she joined the choir. She started having trouble in school. Nothing too alarming, skipping school and hanging with the wrong crowd, but they wanted counseling for her."

This time even I fell silent, reluctant to hear how his peace was shattered. Nervous to learn of the woman I'd reminded him of, at least at first.

"She told me...She said she'd been waiting until she was of age, she said. It wasn't the first time a parishioner had confessed to a crush, but it was the first time she wouldn't take no for an answer. I was uncomfortable... embarrassed. I told her I couldn't speak to her one-on-one anymore. I considered talking to her parents, but then she was nineteen and living on her own. She started having regular sessions with Norm, and I figured the problem was solved."

He pulled me tighter, so tight I couldn't breathe. I stroked him, running my fingers over the goose-bumped skin on his chest.

"I didn't realize it, but she was saying the same things to him. Earning his trust. He thought she loved him. He loved her back. And then she told him that I'd taken advantage of her. That I'd *touched* her even though I hadn't. Not ever."

"I know," I said quietly, though I was sure he wasn't listening. He was tense, sweating, back in the past that hurt him.

"He called the police. They showed up to take me away in handcuffs while he watched from the curb. He wouldn't listen to me, refused to talk about me or see me. I was convicted without ever hearing him speak another word to me."

"I'm sorry," I whispered.

He laughed. "He left the cloth for her. I don't know why, maybe he got suspicious or she just needed to confess, but somehow she ended up telling him the truth. Did she think he would stay with her anyway? He got proof to my lawyer, and they overturned the sentence. In a way, it was too late for me. I was already so fucked up. So many fights...those nights in the ER...I didn't want to be like this. I had to survive. I couldn't..."

"I know. I understand. You couldn't let them."

"The craziest part of the whole thing was when I was released from prison. I got it into my head that he'd be there waiting for me. He would apologize, and I'd already forgiven him. I knew I could never go back to the priesthood, but at least I'd have a friend."

I pulled myself up to face him. "You have a friend."

He tucked a strand of hair behind my head. "I don't deserve one. You, least of all."

"I know I'm pretty great," I said blithely.

He grinned. "A saint."

I rested my forehead against his the way I had in his truck. It brought me closer to him, like I could pull the pain from him and take it into my own body. He did the same for me, really, and we were both conduits for the pain, the currents between us grounding us together. He was the god of thunder, retreating from the world that had rejected him. I was the maiden he'd caught going over the edge, who he'd secreted away in his lair beneath the falls.

"Sometimes I think Norm was a bastard. A stupid, horrible person," he continued, "and I curse him to Hell. Then other days...I knew my friend too well. He believed her. Maybe he was blindsided by her looks or interest in him. Or maybe he was too messed up by what he'd already seen. But either way, he truly believed it of me and that hurt the worst. He's been out there, somewhere, feeling like shit, and I can't stop it. I don't even want to care about that, but I do."

I knew the feeling exactly. My mother wasn't the best, but she hadn't wanted me hurt. She hadn't realized what Allen was doing to me until it was too late. Like Hunter, too late.

And yet, here we both were. Two second chances. Almost a miracle.

"Forgive yourself. It's the only way we can be together."

His lip quirked. "Are you preaching to me, Evie?"

"You know what they say. Those who can, do. Those who can't, preach."

"Do they say that?"

"I have no idea. I've spoken to approximately five people my whole life."

He grinned and kissed me, his lips curved as they

pressed against mine.

It was the first time we had really kissed. His tongue met mine in a sensual meeting, a languid caress followed by another and another. He explored me there as thoroughly as he knew the rest of my body, learning each contour and sweetly sensitive shadow.

Though I felt the usual heat flaring between us, there was no urgency, no expectation that it would turn into more. It touched me that he would spare me sex now when he thought I was weak, but he still didn't quite realize that sex with him strengthened me. It was the most intimate of embraces, a show of support and desire unequaled.

Anticipation warm in my belly, I began to kiss my way down his neck, his chest, and lower, lower, but he stopped me.

Glancing up, I asked, "No?"

He shook his head. "You don't need the added salt intake when you're already dehydrated."

I snorted, then licked the curve of his abs. "You're not that salty."

"Not yet."

My laugh was cut short by the shock of cool water on my belly. He had found that damned washcloth again and he used it to full advantage this time, rubbing it along my body and limbs, over my hardened nipples and down into the soft, damp valley below. He teased me through the rough cloth, dragging me higher to a sharp-sweet crescendo.

I shook in his arms, until he released me and moved downward.

His tongue replaced the cloth, a caress infused with the absolution we needed in the past, a prayer spoken against tender, swollen skin. He took me to heaven and then pulled me back down again with the sharp, swift thrust of him inside me.

It would always be this way, the ecstasy and the pain. They twined together in a path we would walk, unknowing and unseeing, each glad to have found a friend. All I wanted was to be with Hunter wherever his rig should take us. Across the country, around the world.

Like chasing rainbows and capturing each one in the smile it gave us.

Epilogue

In French, the word "salut" means both "hello" and "goodbye."

THE ONLY THING I could see was a long row of red *No Smoking* signs. The cabin had gone dark after dinner—which had tasted surprisingly good. Paneer masala and saffron rice. Not food I expected on Air France, but I didn't mind. I wanted to experience everything the world had to offer, even if it came in small plastic trays from a rolling cart.

My skin had permanently pebbled in the cool airplane. A sandpaper blanket did little to warm me. And the bucket seat had stopped being comfortable around the fifth hour of flight. The man in front of me had reclined his seat so he was almost in my lap. A woman behind me *tap-tap-tapped* her foot against the back of my chair.

And beside me, the little boy managed to flick me with a rubber band. Again.

I tried to give the women on the other side of him a glare that would seem both understanding and firm. Yes, kids would be kids—but if anyone was going to deal with it, shouldn't it be his mother? Unfortunately, she seemed to have fallen asleep.

The boy grinned at me, clearly expecting a response. I probably wasn't allowed to flick him back…

Kids were another thing I didn't know about, like Indian food and international travel. The massive circular X-ray scanners at check-in had seemed impossibly futuristic. Conveyer belts in the middle of hallways and an artistic lighting display overhead, as if O'Hare were a museum instead of an airport. Everything new and exciting and secretly scary.

Flick.

That was enough. I stood and stretched, hoping the mother would wake up from the daggers from my eyes. No such luck. I slipped my phone into my jeans pocket and made my way toward the back, feeling unsteady on my feet. Floor lights lit the way, a miniature runway leading to the back of the plane.

Everyone I passed had their eyes closed, sleeping probably. Some people wore the sleep masks provided by the airline. Others slouched over in their chairs, leaning on their neighbors—or in one case, hanging perilously into the aisle. I nudged the older woman with my hip, careful not to wake her as she slid back into place.

When I looked up, I met the gaze of someone in the very back aisle. I could see the whites of his eyes. A shiver ran through me. Was he some sort of security agent? What had Hunter called them? I had asked tons of questions, making him chuckle. Air marshals. That sounded futuristic too, as if they were shooting through the sky in one-man spaceships. Instead they were ordinary men authorized to carry guns on a plane.

He watched me silently, unblinking. Creepy.

Ignoring the twinge of nerves, I lowered my gaze and continued past him. There was a tiny bathroom that looked mildly suffocating from outside the door. I didn't have to use it anyway; I just couldn't deal with sitting down anymore.

Stop being grumpy. This wasn't my first flight. Small spaces and hard chairs were par for the course on airplanes. I knew the real problem.

I missed Hunter.

Farther back, a small area connected the two parallel aisles. The galley, the flight attendant had called it. They'd said we could come back here for short periods of time if we needed to stretch our legs. Apparently, no one else did. The dim lighting and loud hum of the plane had lulled most everyone to sleep.

Except for Mr. Air Marshal. But then, it was probably his job to stay on alert.

I paced back and forth in the tiny strip of empty space. Was this how it felt to be caged? I had a sudden image of Hunter trapped in a space this small—not only for a few minutes. For years he'd been locked up. Imprisoned. Goosebumps rose on my skin.

A small room was off to the side, some kind of storage closet with a dark blue curtain for a door. The bins all had a special latch, probably so they wouldn't slide open.

I read off the labels, whispering to myself. "Napkins. Sleep Masks. Sporks."

Hah. Sporks.

God, I was tired. I should be sleeping, but I couldn't when I kept getting flicked with a rubber band. Maybe I could fall asleep here, in this tiny space. There was a thin counter. I could wedge myself onto it, somehow strap myself in like I was luggage in a compartment.

A slight smile curved my lips. I was getting silly, the lack of sleep messing with my brain. Even though I knew I shouldn't, I pulled out my phone. It was allowed to be on right now for listening to music or reading, but no phone calls. No signal. I snuck a glance down the aisle— empty, dark—and switched the airplane mode setting to off.

Nothing.

Maybe it wouldn't work. We definitely weren't supposed to be doing this. The flight attendant had made that very clear, along with the pre-flight safety video.

Ah, there they were. Three bars.

Hunter's number was first in the list, most important, but he wouldn't even get this text. *Miss you,* I typed. I pressed the Send button and waited.

Nothing again.

That should have discouraged me, but instead it felt like a blank check. I could say anything. He wouldn't respond, couldn't respond, and it gave me carte blanche to be playful. How much should I say? How graphic could I get? Maybe the boredom pushed me to the edge. Or maybe thinking about Hunter *always* put me on edge.

And thinking about kissing you, I typed. *If you were here, I'd kiss you everywhere.*

Send.

Oh, he'd be mad about that. Naughty texts when he couldn't even get at me. Maybe it wasn't that dirty in the realm of sexting, but he would know how hard it was for me to say the words. He would know exactly what I meant when I said I'd kiss him everywhere—and that *was* dirty. The thought made me laugh under my breath.

A sound came from outside the curtain. I froze, listening. One second passed, then two. The screen of my phone went dark. Only the slightest whisper alerted me to the movement of the curtain. Then someone was inside with me, their heat and presence soaking up all the air. I gasped and shoved myself back into the corner, but there was nowhere to go.

"What are you—"

A hand covered my mouth, cutting off my question. My heart beat too fast, thumping wildly in my chest. Someone had to hear the rapid beat or my harsh breathing. I tried to pull his hand away. My fingers fumbled, clumsy and stiff with terror. The cell phone clattered to the floor, its sound almost completely enveloped by the roar of the engine beneath us.

We were completely insulated back here. And alone.

"I ask the questions." The voice cut through the darkness, low and raspy.

I shook my head, whether in refusal or shock I didn't know. *Let me go,* I tried to say, but my lips couldn't even form the words beneath the force of his palm, my throat didn't make a sound under the threat of his body.

His hand tightened, cutting off the air flow to my nose. I struggled, kicking out and catching him on his leg. He grunted and eased up, enough to let me breath, not enough to let me go. I sank back against the wall, limp with relief, until he picked up my phone.

"What have we here?" Pale blue light from the screen traced broad shoulders and blunt facial features. He looked up. His eyes were impossibly cold, almost reptilian in their unfeeling. *An animal.* "Are you placing a phone call?"

"No," I whispered.

"Let's see." He still spoke low, barely audible above the rushing sound in my ears. "You've sent a text message…two minutes ago. Surely you realize that's not allowed."

"I'm sorry. It was just one. Or two! I won't do it again."

"Two messages. What could be so urgent?" He pressed a button. "Miss you." His gaze met mine over the top of the phone. A wicked light danced in his eyes. He was enjoying this. "And thinking about kissing you."

My cheeks heated beneath his hand.

His smile was sly and calculating. "Lonely, are you?"

I had to look away, humiliated, my innermost thoughts laid bare, flayed open by cold condescension. My stomach tightened into knots. Typing them in the dark, all alone, had been one thing. But I'd never expected this.

"And what's this? *If you were here, I'd kiss you everywhere.* Well, well. Was this so important you had to violate FAA regulations? I wonder what the security personnel in France would have to say about that. They would detain you, at the very least."

A tear leaked from my eye, skating down my cheek and over his hand.

What? Why? My eyes asked the question.

He chuckled. "It's a safety violation, of course. And this? It could be a code. Suspicious activity. And you're the perfect cover, all innocent-looking. But you aren't innocent, are you? Not if you're sending men texts like this."

I looked down, ashamed. He reached behind him and produced a strip of fabric. A sleep mask! He spun me around. I barely had time to register that my mouth was free—to beg, to scream—when he had wrapped the cloth around my mouth like a gag. He tied a knot with efficient, practiced movements. My hands came next, trapped behind my back and handcuffed with more fabric. Had he prepared for this?

Or was he always prepared to capture a girl in the backroom of wherever? I struggled, yanking my hands, testing the ties.

"Shh, stop that." He leaned in close, hands on my hips. His mouth was right against my ear, whispering. Soothing. "Don't fight me. I only want to have some fun with you. To use you for a little while. You don't mind, do you? We both know you want it too."

He reached around and unzipped my jeans. His hand reached inside bluntly, rudely, beneath my panties as if he had every right to be there, in the folds of my sex where the dampness gave me away.

His breath caught. "Oh, that's nice. Very nice."

His forefinger dipped lower into a pool of wetness that grew and grew. I imagined a dark stain on my panties. Would it leak through to my jeans? Would everyone know? He drew the moisture up and over my clit, drawing circles that made me jerk in his hold.

He pinched my clit in reprimand. "Take it. Just accept what you have coming and it won't hurt. Much."

His other hand drew my shirt up, baring my belly and chest to the cool air. My nipples tightened beneath the lace cups of my bra. It hadn't been a comfortable choice for a long plane ride, but I'd wanted the lingerie to be a surprise. I'd imagined undressing for Hunter with the skyline of Paris behind me. Not like this, bound and gagged. Not with cruel fingers shoving the thin lace down, exposing my breasts in the small dark room.

I glanced back to the curtain. Would anyone come here? I doubted anything could be heard, especially not my whimpers or his groans, but maybe a flight attendant would catch us. Would they stop him? They'd have to. And they'd see me like this, half naked. Worse than naked, my clothes bunched and pinching, framing the most shameful parts of me.

"Then you'd better get me off fast." He must have read my mind.

I hung my head, resigned to my fate.

That must have pleased him. He turned me around and pushed me down. The floor was some kind of springy mat, surprisingly comfortable on my knees. I could barely see him in the lack of light. He loomed in front of me, my entire world. But I could hear him. His harsh breathing. The rasp of a zipper.

He didn't even have to say it. *I want to kiss you eve-*

rywhere. I'd written my own debasement.

My mouth and throat were dry when he yanked the gag out of the way. The fleece fabric had taken all the moisture away—but he put it back. With his fingers first, shoving them in, deep enough so I gagged. Then the spongy head of a cock pressed against my lips. I'd been trained well for this. Without a thought, my lips parted, letting him in. He was already slippery, salty, precum coating his cock. The taste of him coated my tongue as he slid deeper.

He cradled the back of my neck, his hands gentle as he held me still for his thrusts. He started shallowly, letting me get used to his rhythm, his size. His hands tightened in my hair. He pressed in deeper, hitting the back of my throat. I gagged, choking, jerking my head away and struggling against the bonds on my wrists as he continued to press deep.

"Don't whine. It's only going to get worse."

And God, he was right. Because then he started to move, fucking my face in a relentless rhythm. I couldn't time my breaths or make a sound. I couldn't even think about stopping him. My world narrowed to his cock in my mouth. I became nothing more than something warm and wet for him to come inside. It didn't even matter if I struggled or passed out as long as he could use me like this.

Everything blurred. I almost didn't register when he

pulled away. My eyes were flooded with tears. My throat felt raw. He didn't have to put the gag back in and he knew it. The last thing I wanted was for someone to find me like this. If the French officials minded my dirty texts, they'd definitely mind me naked and shivering in the back of the plane.

"I was going to come in your mouth, but I can't." He sounded almost apologetic. "I have to get inside that pretty cunt. It was just too wet. I need to feel it around my dick."

I blushed furiously. *Too wet.* As if I'd brought this on myself.

With a gentle shove, he pitched me forward until my face was pressed against the floor. What had seemed soft under my knees felt unyielding against my cheek. The smell of rubber suffused me. How many stewardesses had walked back and forth in their sensible pumps, never knowing what would happen here? How many would continue to do so, stepping on the salt of my tears?

A rough tug pulled my jeans all the way down to my knees. Then he was kneeling behind me. Not between my legs, but with his knees outside mine. I was hogtied, with my hands still tied and my legs locked together by the jeans, unable to even protect myself against what was coming.

"Wait," I said.

He pressed his cock against my opening and slid

home. I bucked against him, twisting away. Even on the inside, my muscles squeezed, trying to push him out. Useless, all of it. He may as well have been a part of the airplane itself, machinery that couldn't be moved by human strength. Even his cock inside me felt more like metal than flesh, hard and invasive.

He groaned. "That's right. Milk me. Make me come."

Those words. I shut my eyes tight, unable to face him—unable to face the floor or the darkness as my body obeyed him. I couldn't *stop* milking him. I couldn't stop making him come, even though I kind of wanted to. That would only prolong this, but I tried anyway. To relax myself, to be passive. But my muscles clenched hard around him, obeying him instead of me, until he gasped and hot liquid bathed my inner walls.

He jerked over me, rocking himself through his orgasm. Even then, I couldn't stop clenching and clenching. It wasn't just for him, I realized. With horror, I acknowledged the feeling inside me. Pure, unstoppable arousal. My cunt wasn't trying to push him out; I was trying to pull him in, deeper, harder, so I could get off too. I felt exposed and dirty, more than the forced blowjob could have done. My own forbidden excitement was the true embarrassment, shining a light on things better left in the dark.

"Shhh." He was at my ear again, soothing me. Only

then did I realize I was crying. Not loose, helpless tears, but quiet sobs that racked my body. I didn't want this. I didn't want to be like this. The shame would never leave me alone, not ever.

He petted my back, stroking me. His other hand slipped underneath to my clit. He didn't circle me this time. Two fingers slid on either side of it, holding still.

"Go ahead," he muttered. "Ride me."

And I did. Shamefully, I did, my hips rocking urgently, rubbing myself off on his hand. It felt almost painful, the sweet friction from his fingers, and I whimpered. He reached under me to where my breasts hung loose. He cupped one and then pinched my nipple. Hard. I came, spilling wetness onto his hand, my moans muffled by the rubber floor and unflinching drone of the plane.

He held me like that a little longer, his fingers warm and still on my clit. Comforting.

When he stood, I tilted to the side, falling against the wall. He found the cabinet marked *Napkins* and cleaned himself and put his clothes to right. Then he did the same for me, wiping my mouth, my sex, and tugging my bra and clothes back into place with a regretful sigh. I let him dress me like a doll, feeling as numb and hollow as one.

He picked up my phone from the shallow ledge. Even the faint light was a shock when I'd been in the dark so long, like squinting into the sun. The screen illuminated his face from below, an almost demonic perspective. He pressed some buttons and then slipped the phone into the pocket of my jeans.

He said nothing to me as he pushed the curtain aside and left. Perhaps there was nothing to say. Everything had been communicated through our bodies, murmurs in a soft caress and shouting in the rough invasion of his cock. A million words had been spoken with every stroke.

I remained in the room, leaning against the wall, as my breathing returned to even.

How long had he been in here with me? A few minutes? An hour? Either way, there was plenty of flight left. Time I would most definitely spend in my seat— just as soon as I could make myself move.

Finally, I pushed off the wall. My legs felt unsteady, as if we were on a ship instead of a plane, rocking to the motion of the waves. I found the restroom and washed my face. A pale face stared out from the small mirror. What was she thinking? Even I didn't know, dazed by exhaustion and recent events.

My hand trailed along the textured plane walls for support. In the open aisle, between the seats, I straightened and forced myself to walk normally. But when I glanced back, a pair of eyes gazed steadily at me. The back row. The Air Marshal.

A shiver ran through me. Fear.

Ducking my head, I continued walking. At least almost everyone else was still sleeping. Even the little boy had fallen asleep, curled up in his seat and mine. I gently nudged him over and let sleep claim me.

✧   ✧   ✧

"WELCOME TO CHARLES De Gaulle Airport. We hope you have a pleasant flight and enjoy your stay in Paris."

I came awake in chunks, registering the seatbelt light dinged off, the rustle as people stood and reached for the overhead compartments. The little boy had stretched out, his head in his mother's lap and his feet in mine.

His mother smiled at me, looking about as bleary as I felt. "Thank you so much for letting us switch seats," she said with a French accent.

"No problem."

"I hope he wasn't any trouble. I think I dozed off early."

"He slept like an angel."

That had been true by the end. And I didn't really mind trading seats. Obviously a child needed to sit with his mother. It was the airline who had assigned them seats on opposite ends of a very large jet.

Straightening, I tried to peek through the curtains at the front of the aisle, trying to catch a glimpse of Hunter. But there were two full sections between us, each with their own galley and restrooms. Passengers were restricted to the facilities in their own section. No mingling across the plane was allowed.

Hunter tended to break rules.

Rules like no sex in the storage closet of an airplane, for example.

I glanced at the back seat. The Air Marshal stretched in the aisle and swung his arms to loosen them. He rifled through a small piece of leather luggage—more of a briefcase. He leaned against the wall, the one I had touched on the way back to my seat, and looked at his phone. I flushed hot and then cold, remembering how my phone had gotten me into trouble last night. Embarrassment wouldn't let me turn it on now, even though it was legal and allowed with the plane at the gate.

The line took forever, as expected since I was almost at the very back, behind the two hundred passengers on the plane. Only a few rows were behind me—and the air marshal waiting patiently in the rear hallway.

His gaze pricked the back of my neck. I stared ahead—which wasn't hard considering how tired the trip had made me. Still, I couldn't rest easy with him just ten feet away. Watching. Knowing.

Did he know what had happened in that storage closet?

I managed a weak smile for the cheery stewardess bidding us goodbye. How did she manage to get any sleep? Maybe there was a special cot somewhere we couldn't see, a miniature dorm room for flight crew only.

They certainly hadn't been in the storage closet.

The temperature dropped twenty degrees in the gangway. My blue hoodie, which had felt perfectly cozy at Chicago's O'Hare terminal, now felt paper thin. Hunter and I would have to pull warmer jackets out of our suitcases before leaving the airport.

But first, I had to find him.

He stood a little bit away from the crowd of disembarking passengers. His expression was inscrutable as I walked up. How did he feel about last night? As for me, I felt sore—and satisfied. They commonly went together where he was concerned. He knew exactly how to get me hot, and it was just our perverse luck that the same things worked for him.

Still, there was a big difference between fumbling in the dark and facing him the morning after. My cheeks heated, and no matter how hard I tried, I couldn't quite meet his gaze.

He chuckled. "Miss me?"

Evil man. "You know I did."

"Bet you were thinking of me."

God, if I let him keep going, he'd tease me until my face burst into flames. "I bet you were thinking of me too."

"Always, sunshine."

Pleasure filled me. Unlike the pleasure from last night, this one wasn't tainted with fear or arousal. This was as wholesome and bright as the nickname he gave me, complete with summertime scents and floating dust motes. Our feelings for each other were pure in a way our base carnality would never be. The sky and the earth, one casting light, the other catching it. Each more complete in the whole.

"Let's grab breakfast," he said, turning to scan the wide terminal corridor. "Do you need a restroom first?"

"No, but I would like breakfast. Something very French. A croissant, maybe, or a baguette."

He grinned. "I'm sure they—"

"Pardon me! Wait, please," a male voice called out, and I froze. Every cell in my body screamed for me to run, but in a crowded airport there was nowhere to go.

The Air Marshal strode up to us. I managed to stop myself from taking a step backward. That would only make me look guilty. But I was guilty. So guilty that being forced was the only way I knew how to have sex. So full of shame every time I enjoyed it anyway.

He knows what we did. I tried to project the thought to Hunter, but he looked completely unfazed.

"Is this your first time in Paris?" the marshal inquired with the faintest accent.

"For her. Not for me, though it has been a while," Hunter answered casually, as if the question had been asked in passing conversation with another tourist instead of an interrogation by a security official.

What if we were detained? Arrested? Hunter didn't look concerned, but then he never did.

The air marshal glanced at my hand. My left hand, with its gold band. "Are you just married then?"

This time the question was clearly directed at me. I opened my mouth but only a mortified squeak came out. My life had plenty of embarrassing moments to choose from. But getting busted for sex on a plane would put the rest of them to shame.

Hunter raised his eyebrows at me. "A month ago."

"Congratulations," the marshal said. "I imagine you'll be visiting the usual places. The Eiffel Tower. Notre Dame."

"Of course. Do you have any recommendations?"

"I do, actually. La Dame de Canton. A restaurant on an old gypsy boat. Mediocre food, relatively speaking, but the ambiance is something to appreciate."

"We'll have to visit then."

"Be sure to request the *boudoir*. It's a small alcove in the back. Very private. I think you would appreciate it."

Hunter raised an eyebrow. A warning? "On your recommendation, then."

The air marshal nodded with surprising deference. "I always enjoy the company of newlyweds. It reminds me of happier times, when I was younger and less divorced."

Hunter barked a laugh before bidding him *au revoir*.

The marshal saluted us and disappeared into the crowd.

"The bastard," Hunter said, but there was no heat behind it.

My chest still felt tight, bands of nerves making it hard to breathe. "He… he *knows*."

"Of course, he knows. That's a voyeur if I ever met one. Hard to blame him, though, considering."

That was awfully level-headed. I narrowed my eyes at him. "I thought you'd be upset."

"That a jaded security guard let us fool around in the storage closet? Nah, not upset. I'd have slipped him something in thanks if it wouldn't have offended him."

Okay then.

AFTER BREAKFAST, IT took us another hour to get into Paris and to our hotel. I was used to a lot of travel by now, but after the expansive, cushy seats of Hunter's truck, the stiff-back chair of the train and the ripped cushions of the cab left something to be desired. The man at the front desk was courteous and faintly judging, so on point I wondered if he was planted to entertain American tourists.

Or then again, maybe he really did feel that way.

Either way, the room itself was beautiful, larger than

I'd been given to expect from the travel guidebooks. A small wall divided the sitting area from the bedroom, which left a spacious area across where the sunlight streamed through filmy curtains. I took a hot shower, admiring the marble floor and overlarge tub in the bathroom.

Now I knew why Hunter had picked this room.

I had a new set of lacy bra and panties to go on under my fresh clothes. For that bit of planning, I deserved a round of applause. A lot of my lingerie would get torn to shreds during our two-week stay here.

At least, I sure hoped so.

When I emerged from the bedroom, Hunter was reclined on the bed. He tossed his phone aside. "Come closer."

I planned to jump him, just jump directly on top of him and tussle for control. I loved it when he won, so I gave him every opportunity. But before I could make it to the bed, he said, "Now stop. That's perfect."

"Perfect for what?"

"For you to show me those lacy panties you had on." When I blushed he added, "You're lucky I didn't rip them off you right there on the plane. Shove them in your mouth and make you taste our own come."

God. I clenched my thighs together, trying to ease the ache that started every time he talked like that. His grin was pure devilry, smug and tempting.

Two could play at this game.

"I don't know what you mean," I said, feigning innocence. "I've already changed."

"Then show me what you're wearing now," he growled.

I pulled my jeans and top off as slowly as I could without being silly. There was only so seductive rumpled travel clothes could get. But my silk bra with its little pink flowers—oh, those would do nicely. He sucked in a breath when he saw it. And my panties. Not only did they match, but the panel was still damp from his come. It leaked out of me for hours after he came inside me, a musky reminder of what we'd done. He came a lot, copiously.

And often too.

"Do you mean *these* panties?" I asked.

I'd found that dirty talk didn't need to be particularly clever to turn Hunter on. In fact, simple worked best. *Please. Do it like that.* And my coup de grace had been a quiet *No, no, I can't take any more* during a particularly rough scene that had made him come for what felt like hours.

Hunter grunted something like assent. "Get over here."

His hand absently rubbed himself through his jeans, a sign of dwindling patience. Soon enough he'd grab me, fling me to the floor, and have his dirty way with me. An excellent recipe for orgasms if I ever heard one. But this time around, I had a different idea.

My panties slipped over my hips and down to the floor. I unclasped my bra and held it against my chest for a moment before letting it fall. But instead of leaving the lacy fabric on the Aubusson rug, I hooked it with my forefinger.

When he reached for me, I stayed his hand. His eyebrows shot up. I could see the questions behind his brown eyes. Was it a game? Did I want him to overpower me?

I shook my head slightly. *Not this time.*

With a quick movement, I ripped the panties down their seam, lace tearing with a quiet *snip*. He and I both stared at the scrap of fabric in shock. Well, I'd imagined him tearing through my panties, not me, but this would be better. Just this once.

"Shall I?" I asked softly.

His eyes blazed. He looked...furious. But his breath quickened and his cock bulged as thick as ever through the jeans. Oh, he would like this. Just this once, and maybe a few more times, just to be sure.

I straddled his thighs and tied the panties over his mouth. Reaching around, I fastened the bra into a kind of makeshift handcuffs. The same way he'd tied me up last night. The whole time, I was acutely aware of the raw power between my legs and within my embrace. I only tied him up because he let me.

But then again, that was why he tied me up too.

"Good?" I asked.

His eyes were flames of frustration, of desire. He wanted to attack me but the pink-flower bonds and my wish to do this held him bound. "Poor man," I whispered, trailing a finger down his temple. It must be hard for him to give in, even for a little while.

I would have to give him a reward.

The ridge in his jeans tempted me. I wanted to suck on the spongy head, to flutter my tongue at the tip, to drive him crazy when he couldn't take control, couldn't thrust.

Although maybe he still would. His hips were already moving, without any stimulation to his cock. He was fucking the air, overexcited from just seeing me naked and getting tied up.

He was so damned responsive.

Sucking him off would hardly return the favor from last night. I'd already done that. A good time for all, but I knew what he wanted. What he needed. Gently, carefully, I helped him lie flat on the bed. It didn't look easy. He had to lie on his hands, which were still bound behind him. However, the discomfort was part of the allure. I wanted everything for him. Even pain.

And besides, he looked so good spread out, broad chest pressed up into the air, flat abs trailing into his jeans. He looked like one of the Greek statues in the guidebook for the Louvre. We'd get to see the artwork soon, but this was even better—marble turned man.

I shoved the panty-gag aside and pressed my fingers into his mouth. "Suck."

He bit me. Of course he did. I had to pinch his side until he let go. We both knew he could have overpowered me at any moment. With his body, with his teeth. But he didn't, and that was a greater gift than a shuddering forbidden orgasm. Greater even than a honeymoon in France.

I straddled his face and knelt over him. "Get to work. And no biting or you won't like what happens next."

He licked me eagerly, belying the fierce defiance in his eyes. But no, I read that wrong. It was the game we played that made it look like reluctance. As his eyes fell shut, I saw only triumph and bliss. He'd asked to do this so many times. And each one, I had refused. He could make me, but it wasn't the same. Wasn't the same at all as me tying him down and fucking him with my face.

Reaching down, I tugged on his hair, hard enough that he'd feel the sting. "There's a good boy." His eyes snapped open at that, twinkling with warning.

I laughed. "You're going to make me pay for this, aren't you? I can't wait."

We stayed in our hotel room the next two days, ordering ridiculous quantities of room service while he showed me all the ways he could make me suffer. I expected a complaint to make us keep quiet, especially after a few choice times. But I guess everyone knows what to expect from newlyweds, even stuffy bellhops. Even jaded air marshals.

Even rough and tumble truckers from Texas knew what happened on a honeymoon, and Hunter made it hurt so good.

* * *

Thank you so much for reading this dark and twisted book!

And now you can read about Hunter and Evie's daughter…

I'm stepping off a nine-hour flight when it happens. A white van. A dark hood. Every woman's worst nightmare. Now I'm trapped in an abandoned church. The man who took me says I won't be hurt. The man in the cell next to me says that's a lie. I'll fight with every ounce of strength, but there are secrets in these walls. I'll need every single one of them to survive.

Sign up for the VIP Reader List to find out when I have a new book release:
www.skyewarren.com/newsletter

Join my Facebook group, Skye Warren's Dark Room, for exclusive giveaways and sneak peeks of future books. Continue reading for an excerpt from DIAMOND IN THE ROUGH…

* * *

I WAKE UP with my face pressed into a warm, muscular shoulder. The scruff of his jaw leaves a soft ache on my forehead. My lips feel slightly moist, as if I possibly drooled while I was asleep. Oh God. Embarrassing. Everything about this is embarrassing. Especially the fact that I don't know this man. My hand rests on his arm, only a few inches away from his thigh. I pull back, but the belt and the arm of the seat conspire to keep me close. "Sorry," I say, breathless. "I'm sorry."

A crooked smile with a hint of dazzling white teeth. Dear Lord, men have no business looking this handsome. Especially not on hour eight of a transatlantic flight. "I never mind sleeping with a beautiful woman. Not that I was doing much sleeping."

My cheeks burn. Is he flirting with me? *Of course he's not, Tillie.*

He takes pity on me. "Now it's my turn to apologize. That was inappropriate."

I run a hand over my face. Nope, not a dream. "I think we're past inappropriate. In fact I should probably start keeping a toothbrush at your place."

That earns me a quiet laugh. No one should look glamorous in the economy section, but the light glints off his golden hair. His shirtsleeves and slacks are exactly the comfortable shade of rumpled. His loafers still shine. Instead of seeming out of place among the scratchy fabric and cramped seating, he makes it seem like a stylish place. People in business class would clamor to sit next to him if they could see him. Maybe he's some kind of model who the airline uses for their in-flight magazine.

In contrast I feel brittle, as if the stale air has been stripping moisture from my skin while I slept. I wipe my eyes, trying to focus. The faint scent of coffee wafts from the back of the plane.

"Well, I appreciate the use of your shoulder."

"Qu'est-ce qu'une jolie fille comme toi fait seule?"

The melody of his voice sinks into my bones. His meaning does not. The pocket dictionary I picked up at the airport taught me how to ask for the bathroom. I doubt that's what he wants from me. "Sorry," I say, sheepish. "I don't speak French."

Blonde eyebrows go up. "Non? Who let you go off on this vacation without a guide?"

"It's not a vacation." I'm reluctant to share my reasons for buying the first ticket out of Kentucky. Then again I did just use him as a pillow without his consent. "I'm looking for someone."

"A lucky man."

I don't correct him. My sister is neither male nor lucky. If there's a hole, she'll fall into it. If there's a rake, she'll step on it and run straight into the pole—cartoon style. It's almost impressive her record for getting into scrapes. Her trip to Paris was basically doomed to end in disaster. I had a thousand dollars ready to wire her and the number for the embassy in case she lost her passport. I was prepared for some mishap. I wasn't prepared for her to go completely missing.

A flight attendant appears with a cart, serving watery coffee and an over-sweet muffin on a plastic plate. I scarf both of them down, because I'm starving. I moan in relief.

My neighbor takes a sip of his coffee with a pained expression. "For this you make sex sounds? A proper cup of French coffee and some crepes. That's what you need."

This banter thing is actually fun. "Do you make sex sounds for crepes?"

"Why don't you find out? I could show you around, until you meet this mystery man."

My smile fades. He's really hitting on me. What a strange twenty-four hours this has turned out to be. "That sounds lovely, and really, any other time…"

He puts a hand to his heart. "Don't explain, ma chere."

That was a lie, of course. Any other time I wouldn't be on this airplane. We never would have met. The thought gives me the courage to ask, "What's your name?"

"Charles." He says the name in that fluid accent. *Shar-el.* It seems almost obscene, the way his tongue caresses the syllables. "Charles Bisset."

"Matilda," I say in response, though I manage to stop myself before I share my last name. He doesn't seem like the type of man with a brood of children at home. He's too movie-star handsome to imagine in a real world setting. I don't want to take the chance.

"I'm so glad to meet you, Matilda," he says with such warmth it feels real. Not just something that people say to strangers they'll never see again.

"Same," I manage, even though I'm not the same. I'm different, different, different. Cold. Scared. Unable to feel anything but dread. I'm not in France for a vacation. I'm here to find my sister.

The pilot comes over the speakers. We're starting our final descent. I make sure my seatbelt is buckled, that my tray is secured, that my seat is in its upright position. And then I close my eyes, blocking out the fight attendant and the gilded man beside me. I block out everything except sensation. I'm thirty thousand feet in the air and dropping. Is this what it feels like to fly? No, because this feels like nothing. Or maybe that's how birds feel. My characters would know. Children always know. And when I'm writing them, when I'm Matilda Frank, beloved author, I can feel the world through their eyes.

✧   ✧   ✧

THE AIRPORT ITSELF feels sleepy, heavy shades drooping

over dark windows. Workers push large floor cleaners across a floor that's lost its gloss. Every other restaurant has bars over its entrance. Closed. Good thing I'm not hungry.

It's four a.m. The embassy opens in a few hours.

A lone suitcase circles the conveyor belt. A family with two children appear with a large stuffed elephant that probably needed its own seat. A selection of individual men and women, probably business travelers. A couple who are leaning on each other. Honeymoon? We're all too exhausted to do anything more than stare straight ahead.

The man from the plane doesn't show up. Charles Bisset. I don't know whether I'm disappointed not to see him again. He would have made small talk, and I hate small talk.

Except when it's with handsome strangers, apparently.

Then even talking about the weather would make a little fire pitch inside my stomach.

He probably only brought a carry on. Except he hadn't pulled one down from the overhead bins. He'd only had a leather briefcase. Strange, even for someone traveling light.

A loud buzzing sound heralds the arrival of our luggage. They slide down the chute, stacking on each other in clumps like a poorly played game of Tetris. After a full revolution of the carousel, my purple bag appears. I grasp it and pull, almost falling backwards.

Signs lead the way through customs and border control. I'm snapped at in rapid French for not checking the right box on the form. And then I'm finally free to find the exit. A big blue sign proclaims TAXI. I pull my luggage along the rubbery floor, eager for a breath of fresh air. A block of exhaust envelopes me. The crowd of people shout and wave their arms, a stark contrast to the languor inside the airport. These aren't travelers. That registers first. They don't have luggage. They're wearing jackets and holding signs. Protestors. Something about Uber. A row of yellow and black taxis don't appear to be moving. A group of men surround a black Escalade, pushing, pushing, and I let out a shriek that no one hears. A window breaks, and they cheer.

"They're on strike," comes a low voice behind me, and I gasp. Charles gives me an apologetic smile. "The taxi drivers. Only a matter of time before they get violent."

I watch them rock the Expedition back and forth on its wheels. "That's not violent?"

"More violent," he amends. "It'll be hell getting out of here"

Anxiety grips my chest. "What should I do?"

He pauses, seeming almost embarrassed. "You could get a train. Or… look, I hesitate to say this. I don't want you to think I'm hitting on you. Again, that is. But I have a towncar waiting. One fo those things you schedule before the trip. They wait in a different lane than taxis."

Relief is a steaming cup of coffee on a terrible morning. "God, that sounds—no, I couldn't. I mean it sounds wonderful, but I couldn't inconvenience you that way."

He nods, once. Then turns, as if to walk away. Then looks back. "Where are you going? It might be on the way to where I'm going. Maybe."

Hope sparks inside me. "The embassy. The American embassy."

A pause. He rubs a large palm across his jaw, and I can hear the scrape of his growth from here. "I believe that's in central Paris. Where I'm heading. Listen, are you in some kind of trouble? We could look for a cop around here. I'm sure we can find one."

That's what decides me, that genuine note of concern in his voice. "No, I'm not in trouble. It's my sister. She's been missing a week already. I have to go to the embassy."

His brown eyes soften. "I can get you to central Paris. Then you can grab a cab."

"Thank you. God." A stone smashes a window. "So much."

He takes the handle of my suitcase before I can object. Then he's wheeling it over a bumpy sidewalk crossing. I struggle to keep up with his long strides. We round a corner, and everything becomes suddenly quiet. It's almost eerie, the way sound doesn't travel around this building. As if the riot a few yards away was a dream.

There's not a neat row of black towncars. There's only a lonely road. And a dumpster.

I do a little skip to eat up the pavement. "Are you sure this is the right way?"

"I'm sure," he calls back, not slowing for an instant.

Nervous energy hits my body like I've run into a wall. Sparks in my ches. A thud at the base of my skull. I suck in air through a straw. I can't trust him, this Charles Bisset. That might not even be his name. My step falters, but he has my suitcase. All my things. My clothes. Pictures of my sister. Her birth certificate. What if I take it from him? What if I rip it out of his hand and run back to the cabs? Part of me feels ridiculous for even thinking it. He's done nothing wrong. All he did was walk fast. That's not a crime. Twenty four years of social conditioning tell me to act normal. Act nice. The persistent rat-tat-tat of my heart warns me that something is wrong.

"Excuse me? Mr. Bisset. *Charles.* Wait."

He doesn't wait. He just keeps walking, and that's when I know, when I *know*, that I'm in trouble. I stop mid-step. I need what's in the suitcase. How can I make my way in a foreign city without clothes? But I can't follow this man into—where? I take a step back.

The screech of a tire snaps me to attention. A white van bumps onto the curb. The man inside wears a black ski mask. Time slows to a crawl. Gravel sprays from the thick black tires. The protestors dim to a low roar. *They won't hear me if I scream.* I turn toward Charles, as if he might protect me. And for a moment, he does. He pulls me close to him, shielding me. He murmurs in my ear, "Don't fight, mon cherie. It will only make this harder for you.'"

My eyes widen. Then something black and thick covers my head. Hands drag me toward the van, and I fight, blind and in shock, lashing out at nothing before my arms are caught behind my back. Then I'm shoved roughly into something in motion. Something hard hits my face. The floor. I'm slammed to the side. A sharp pain behind my head. And then darkness.

My EYES OPEN to pitch black.

I wait for my bedroom to come into focus. Nothing happens. This is the complete kind of darkness, the kind without even shadows. My lungs burn, as if I've been holding my breath. I gulp down damp and moldy air. I curl my fingers against stone. Faintly slick. Biting cold.

Where am I?

Memories drop into my mind like rain in a puddle. I

remember the long flight and fear for my sister. I remember the man with the movie star smile.

A shudder works its way through my body, lingering in aches and bruises, waking up pain as it goes. I move myself to a sitting position with a soft groan. The floor feels slightly uneven, almost like a natural rock formation. A cave or something.

I crawl forward. Something hard meets my face. My fists close around iron bars.

Not completely natural, then.

Charles Bisset. *Shar-el.* Why did he take me? Because I'm a tourist? Maybe he thought I'd have money. That's no reason to take me, only my bags.

Or maybe he recognized me as the famous children's book author. Except that the only person who could pay ransom is my sister, and she's missing.

There's no other reason he would take me.

Isn't there? The soft voice inside my head knows exactly why a man would take a woman. He asked me out, didn't he? He asked to show me around the city. I said no.

He doesn't take rejection well.

The darkness closes in on me, it becomes a tactile force, squeezing my lungs. I don't want to stay here, in this pitch black prison. I *can't* stay here. There's no oxygen. I gasp through the fist around my throat. I'm going to die here, before Charles can even touch me, and that seems almost like a gift, except that the body fights anyway. It wants to live.

The darkness closes in on me.

"Easy," comes a voice from the inky void. I choke on air. "Easy there," he says again.

"Charles," I gasp out. It's twisted that I'd actually be relieved to have him here. Anything is better than being alone right now. Even the presence of my captor.

There's quiet.

I'm not alone in the dark, though. My fists curl around iron. "Answer me."

"I'm not Charles." And he's not. He's missing the fluid accent. He says the name the American way, with harsh syllables. His voice is completely different—lower, more blunt, gravelly like the broken concrete underneath me.

"Who are you?" Was he the driver of the van? Or someone else?

"I'm no one." Shadows curl around his rough voice. His presence settles into my skin, deeper than the dust, farther than the cold. He's someone, this stranger.

Want to read more? Diamond in the Rough is available on Amazon, iBooks, Barnes & Noble, and other book retailers!

BOOKS BY SKYE WARREN

Endgame trilogy & Masterpiece duet
The Pawn
The Knight
The Castle
The King
The Queen

Trust Fund duet
Survival of the Richest
The Evolution of Man

Underground series
Rough
Hard
Fierce
Wild
Dirty
Secret
Sweet
Deep

Stripped series

Tough Love

Love the Way You Lie

Better When It Hurts

Even Better

Pretty When You Cry

Caught for Christmas

Hold You Against Me

To the Ends of the Earth

Standalone Books

Wanderlust

On the Way Home

Beauty and the Beast

Anti Hero

Escort

For a complete listing of Skye Warren books, visit www.skyewarren.com/books

About Skye Warren

Skye Warren is the New York Times bestselling author of dangerous romance such as the Endgame trilogy. Her books have been featured in Jezebel, Buzzfeed, USA Today Happily Ever After, Glamour, and Elle Magazine. She makes her home in Texas with her loving family, sweet dogs, and evil cat.

Sign up for Skye's newsletter:
www.skyewarren.com/newsletter

Like Skye Warren on Facebook:
facebook.com/skyewarren

Join Skye Warren's Dark Room reader group:
skyewarren.com/darkroom

Follow Skye Warren on Instagram:
instagram.com/skyewarrenbooks

Visit Skye's website for her current booklist:
www.skyewarren.com

COPYRIGHT

This is a work of fiction. Any resemblance to actual persons, living or dead, business establishments, events or locales is entirely coincidental. All rights reserved. Except for use in a review, the reproduction or use of this work in any part is forbidden without the express written permission of the author.